"WHAT ARE YOU RUNNING AWAY FROM?" JOYCE ASKED.

"A sexy-as-hell, teacher–team manager who's been calling the plays all night," Ben replied.

"Afraid of the ball?" she boldly tormented.

Ben threaded his fingers into the silky length of her hair, tilting her head until their lips met.

"Still scared?" she whispered. His lips hovered over hers as though making a momentous decision.

Sizzling seconds later, he answered, "Petrified. I don't like bossy women, Joyce MacIntyre. They're more trouble than they're worth. When I'm attracted to one"—he turned and quickly moved through the door—"I run."

"Quitter!" she yelled at his retreating back.

CANDLELIGHT ECSTASY CLASSIC ROMANCES

FUN AND GAMES

Anna Hudson

A CANDLELIGHT ECSTASY ROMANCE®

Published by
Dell Publishing Co., Inc.
1 Dag Hammarskjold Plaza
New York, New York 10017

ISBN: 0-440-12763-7

Printed in the United States of America

February 1987

10 9 8 7 6 5 4 3 2 1

WFH

Dedicated to the managers and coaches who have made baseball my son's favorite sport.

To Our Readers:

We have been delighted with your enthusiastic response to Candlelight Ecstasy Romances®, and we thank you for the interest you have shown in this exciting series.

In the upcoming months we will continue to present the distinctive sensuous love stories you have come to expect only from Ecstasy. We look forward to bringing you many more books from your favorite authors and also the very finest work from new authors of contemporary romantic fiction.

As always, we are striving to present the unique, absorbing love stories that you enjoy most—books that are more than ordinary romance. Your suggestions and comments are always welcome. Please write to us at the address below.

Sincerely,

The Editors
Candlelight Romances
1 Dag Hammarskjold Plaza
New York, New York 10017

FUN AND GAMES

CHAPTER ONE

"My ol' man ain't gonna like me havin' no woman baseball coach."

"Manager," Joyce MacIntyre succinctly corrected, grinning at the swaggering eight-year-old boy. The moment she'd introduced herself to the members of the Little League baseball team, they'd groaned in unison. Only one child appeared ecstatic with the news, a girl.

"All the other teams have a daddy managing their team," another boy piped. "How come we got a mommy?"

" 'Cause you're lucky!" Joyce held up her hands to stop the loud moaning noises. She'd expected this reaction. In fact, when asked to volunteer, she'd initially refused. Only when the league president, Cliff James, told her that they'd have to drop a team for lack of a manager had she finally agreed. "And because none of the fathers on this team could spare the time away from their jobs to be a full-time manager."

"We ain't gonna win no games," the first child

said, tossing his new glove on the ground. "I'm quittin'."

"Me, too."

Another glove bit the dust.

"Now, wait a minute," Joyce protested, certain she'd be standing in front of a pile of gloves within moments. "I watched you guys try out. You're hand picked. The best."

The boys grinned at the unexpected praise.

"Oh, yeah?" the protester argued, kicking his glove toward her feet. "Then how come we gotta *girl* on our team?"

"Stacy?" From the worn condition of the leather baseball glove Stacy held tucked under her arm, Joyce automatically guessed that Stacy could play circles around most of these boys. "How about throwing a few?"

"Yes, ma'am." Stacy hustled to the bag on first base. With a mischievous twinkle in her cornflower-blue eyes, she shouted, "Fire 'em in. I can catch anything."

Joyce pointed to the self-proclaimed leader, then stooped and picked up his glove. "What's your name?"

"Sonny. Sonny Hawkins."

Sam Houston couldn't have said it louder or prouder, Joyce mused, tossing the boy's glove, watching his quick reflexes as he caught it. "How about warming up with Stacy?"

"She'll just have to chase it." Sonny chortled.

"Maybe. Move on over to home plate and let's

12

find out." Joyce put her arm across the shoulder of the smallest child. "The rest of you move away from the baseline."

Joyce watched Stacy slip her glove on her hand. Knees bent, glove at the waist, Stacy waited. Saying a short, silent prayer, Joyce hoped her judgment on picking out a natural athlete hadn't failed her. Sonny's excessive windup would have made a major league pitcher jealous. The hard ball whizzed from his hand, beelining down the baseline. Stacy caught it, grinned, and fired it back.

"Wow!" the child whose shoulder Joyce had her arm around gasped in awe.

"Can't you throw it harder?" Stacy jeered.

"I was just takin' it easy on you 'cuz you're a girl," Sonny yelled. "I didn't think you'd catch it."

His second pitch was wild, high. Stacy leaped upward, snagging the ball. "Good thing this is five-pitch so the coach gets to pitch. You just knocked the batter in the head!"

Joyce walked over to the equipment bag and dumped several new balls on the ground, tempting the remaining boys. "How about the rest of you?"

The boys scurried toward the balls, choosing partners, spacing themselves as they lined up along the first and third base line. Joyce heaved a sigh of relief. She unobtrusively mingled with the players, learning their names and gauging their skills.

"Keep your eye on the ball!" she shouted toward Stevie just as his partner lobbed a ball. Daisy picker, she mused good-naturedly, knowing every team had at least one. Stevie would be the fielder who was more interested in what was growing on the ground than in the ball coming toward him.

Inwardly smiling, she walked behind the six boys on the third base line. How many times had she heard her dad shout the same instruction? Too many to count. Each spring, fathers and sons trooped out to the baseball field with military precision. Armed with gloves, balls, and wooden bats, they competed. Slugger, southpaw, grand slammer became part of the boys' vocabulary. Heroes such as Babe Ruth, Joe DiMaggio, and Jose Cruz were emulated by the way a boy held his bat or pitched the ball.

Back then, Joyce had been one of the first girls to join a league in her hometown of Ralston, Texas.

Facing these six- to eight-year-olds as their manager was a breeze compared to being accepted in a previously all-boy league. Joyce knew what to expect then, and now. The men couldn't stop the girls from participating, but they sure could make it miserable for them. By the end of the first week of practice, she'd begged her father to let her drop off the team.

14

She could almost see herself sitting on her dad's lap, wailing, "Hardball is for boys. Softball, Dad, I want to play softball!"

Her dad adamantly refused, saying, "It's a man's world, honey. You'll have to compete with them later. Might as well learn to play hardball early."

She had. Over the years, she'd kept her eye on the ball and kept her goals in sight. She'd learned that team play often required sacrifice hitting. It took shrewd judgment to determine when to bunt and when to go for the homer. At twenty-nine, she'd felt the glory of winning and the devastation of defeat. And, she'd learned about striking out in the game of hardball. The game of life.

Mentally, Joyce shrugged as she caught a stray ball barehanded. "Okay, kids. One lap around the bases, then line up and I'll pass out your uniforms. Hustle! First person across home plate gets to pick his or her favorite number."

Glancing toward the wooden bleachers, Joyce saw several parents waiting to pick up their children. She waved and flashed them the thumbs-up sign. Joyce felt as though she were stealing second on a bunt ball. She'd made first base by getting past the kids; the parents were second base.

It didn't take a mental giant to match Sonny Hawkins with his father. One thumb hooked through the belt loops of his faded jeans, scuffed boots on his feet, scowl on his face, Mr. Hawkins charged toward her carrying the box of uniforms under his arm.

"It's god awful havin' the team mother in charge of the first practice. Couldn't your husband make it today, little lady?"

"I'm the manager. Mr. Hawkins, I presume?"

The box thudded to the ground between them. Bubba Hawkins's jaw dropped as his eyes flickered over her from her near-white hair to her near-white sneakers. "A girl manager?"

Gritting her teeth behind her smile, Joyce joked, "Girl? Why, thanks, Mr. Hawkins. I haven't been called 'girl' since I had my braces removed."

"When was that? Last year? I'll bet you still have to show an ID to buy cigarettes."

Joyce glanced at her attire. Her blue shorts and white top matched the regulation gym uniform the girls at her school wore to her gym class. But she wasn't about to make explanations to this chauvinist. Getting from the neighboring school district to the baseball field left little time to primp. And there was no reason to change out of her gym clothes to coach baseball. The thick, French plaited braid swinging across her shoulders down to her waist subtracted from her age also. She swiped her hand over the bridge of her nose knowing her freckles added to her youthful appearance.

Biting her tongue to keep a scathing retort in her mouth, she stepped back from home plate.

16

Stacy slid between them, then agilely rolled to her feet.

"Hi, Bubba! Whaddaya think of our manager? Pretty keen, huh? Can't wait till Uncle Ben meets her."

Before Bubba could respond, Stacy dashed to the fence behind home base, frantically searching for her uncle.

"Peachy keen," Bubba muttered.

"Just for the record, Bubba. Athletes don't smoke," Joyce tossed over her shoulder as she bent down and ripped open the cardboard box that contained the team's shirts.

"Stacy, what number do you want?"

"Number one!"

"Hrmph!" Bubba authoritatively cleared his throat. "Girls get first choice? My boy has had number one both years he's played."

Straightening, Joyce smiled, and said in a honey-sweet voice, "Sonny crossed the plate fourth." Much to her surprise, Stevie crossed second, and Jacob, the smallest child on the team, followed close on Stevie's heels.

"Every other manager lets the best player choose first," Bubba corrected. "My boy has been shortstop both years."

Joyce arched one blond eyebrow. "Looks as though Sonny is going to have a little competition for that position. Stevie, what number do you want?"

"Gotta number thirteen?"

"Sorry. Twelve players, twelve shirts."

Stevie groaned. "Aw shucks, with a thirteen plastered on my back my folks wouldn't expect much. Twelve will have to do."

Joyce dug to the bottom of the pile and handed him a T-shirt. As she handed the shirt to Steve, she noticed the bold lettering of the sponsor on the back: JOISTS AND STUDS. In smaller letters, she read, FRAMING CONTRACTOR. A small giggle passed between her parted lips.

Sonny grabbed a shirt off the top of the pile and began singsonging, "I'm a Stud! I'm a Stud! I'm a Stud!"

A wide smile stretched Bubba's face. "That's my boy."

Controlling herself to keep her eyes from rolling heavenward, Joyce called, "Who's number three?"

Within minutes all the players had their shirts. The parents semicircled around Joyce, examining the peacock-blue shirts, laughing at the builders' apropos choice of company name. On the fronts of the shirt ASTRO blazed in orange and red, three-inch letters.

"Hey, kids. Pipe down. I need to talk to your parents." Joyce raised to her full five-foot-five-inch height. "We need volunteers. Two coaches, one score keeper, and a team mother."

The parents' groans sounded much like the earlier groans of their children.

From the back of the group, Joyce heard some-

18

one mutter, "We have a woman manager, maybe we ought to have a team *daddy*."

"I'll be the team mother if I don't have to collect any money," one mother offered. "And I won't be responsible for drafting people for the concession stand."

"I'll collect the money and set up the concession stand schedule," the mother holding Jacob's hand volunteered. "Everybody takes a turn. We don't have to work when we're scheduled to play. Bring your wallets to the opening game. That's when I'll collect the snow-cone money."

"And the picture money," the first woman added.

"And the individual trophy money," Stevie's mother said. "Don't forget the end of the year pizza party money, either."

Joyce greatly appreciated having two experienced Little League mothers step in. "Anyone volunteer to keep score?"

Silence.

"Anybody know *how* to keep score?"

Silence.

"The league officials are persnickety about marking down every move the kids make. I don't mind . . ."

Joyce grabbed the hesitant father's hand. "Thanks, Mister . . ."

"Carleton. Jim Carleton. Rick's dad."

Bubba pounded Jim on the back hard enough to lurch the smaller man forward. "Good man.

Certified Public Accountant ought to be good enough for those officials."

Noting the gleam of anticipation in Bubba's eyes, Joyce dreaded asking for the next volunteer. "Coaches?"

Stacy broke through the circle. "Uncle Ben said he'd help, but the old sidewinder isn't here. He promised me that if I'd sign up for the team, he'd coach."

"What's your uncle's name? I'll call him tonight." Joyce picked up her clipboard from the ground.

"Ben Williams. Our number is 555-8884."

Joyce scanned the faces of the other parents. "We need one more coach." *Don't volunteer,* she thought, avoiding eye contact with Bubba Hawkins. *Please, someone, anyone!*

"Mr. Hawkins," Jim Carleton said, "didn't you coach one of the major league teams when your older son played?"

Joyce wanted to protest, but couldn't. Major league boys were young adolescents; minor league boys were children. Would Bubba realize the difference between the two age groups? She doubted it.

"Yeah. The Rebel team I coached were champions that year," Bubba bragged.

Joyce was holding her breath. She wanted a winning team, every coach did. However, learning the skills and good sportsmanship were equally important.

"Why don't you volunteer?" Jacob's mother asked.

Bubba strutted to the front of the semicircle. "Well, now. I'm a busy man."

He wants to be begged, Joyce deduced, watching Bubba rub the whiskers on his chin as though giving second thought to how much the team needed him.

Unable to stop herself, she said, "Maybe someone else—a mother, perhaps?"

Two mothers physically shrank back into the ranks of the group. Blank expressions on the faces of the other mothers told Joyce she couldn't expect any one of them to volunteer. They'd support her from behind . . . way behind.

"But I might be able to work the practices into my schedule," Bubba reconsidered aloud. "The company I work for likes to see their executives active in community sports."

"C'mon, Dad," Sonny wheedled. "You've never coached my team. With a woman manager, we're going to need your help."

Encouraged by his son and the parents, Bubba grinned. "Well, if you folks really want me to coach . . ."

"We do!" several parents chorused.

"In that case, I guess I'll have to let you draft me." Bubba chuckled, rubbing the expanse of belly that hung over his belt buckle. "I learned in the marines not to volunteer."

Terrific! A war hero! He looks as though he ex-

pects to be raised to their shoulders and carried around the field!

The odds against having parental backing were stacking up against Joyce in favor of Bubba Hawkins. Given half a chance, she knew that Bubba was the type who would encourage the boys to take a lead off the base before the ball crossed the plate. She'd be teaching the rules, while Bubba taught the boys how to get around them.

Joyce had to establish which of them would make the final decisions.

"Welcome to the coaching staff, Bubba. As manager, I'll be contacting you and Stacy's uncle to arrange a pre-practice meeting. We'll want to talk over which skills we'll be working on at the next practice."

Bubba shook his head in protest. "Can't. You and Ben get together if you have to. I'll just show up at the practices. Like I said, I'm too busy for social get-togethers."

"But, we need . . ."

Bubba turned toward his son. The parents parted, right in the center, as Sonny and his dad headed for the parking lot. "You and me can teach those kids how to hit home runs, right Sonny? Can't have you stuck on a losing team."

Unable to detain the parents any longer, Joyce said, "We practice on Thursdays. Five o'clock sharp. Thanks for coming today."

Stacy lingered, muttering as she helped Joyce

pick up the practice balls and toss them into the equipment bag.

"You won't let Uncle Ben weasel out of his promise, will you?" Stacy asked, drawing the canvas bag closed with a tug.

From the slightly abashed expression on Stacy's face, Joyce suspected Stacy volunteered Uncle Ben without his consent. "Does your uncle usually keep his promises?"

"Yeah, he's big on being fair." The tip of Stacy's baseball cleats dug into the chalked baseline. "He did promise . . . sort of."

"Sort of?"

White dust puffed up as Stacy nervously kicked it. "He said he'd think about it. I know what that means. By the time he's finished thinking about it, the season will be over."

"Maybe your dad or mom . . ."

"I'm a orphan. Uncle Ben's raised me since I was a baby."

Joyce had all she could do to keep from hugging Stacy. Regardless of how loving an uncle she had, growing up without a mom and dad was tough. She wondered what tragedy took their lives. "I'm sorry."

Shrugging, Stacy looked up at Joyce. "It's real important to me to have Uncle Ben coach. Do you think you can convince him?"

"I'll do my best." Seeing Stacy's triumphant smile, Joyce stipulated, "But I can't promise."

"Uncle Ben says that doing my best is good

23

enough for him. I guess you doing your best is good enough for me." Stacy wheeled around when she heard her name called from across the field. "I gotta run. That's the housekeeper, Mrs. Shane, yellin' for me to come home. See ya."

Joyce waved, then heaved the equipment bag to her shoulder and headed in the opposite direction toward the parking lot. The first practice had gone relatively well. The kids halfway accepted her. The parents hadn't passed out when she introduced herself. She had two competent team mothers and a reluctant scorekeeper. So much for the positive side of the day, she silently tabulated.

Bubba Hawkins condescending to coach still stuck in her craw. He manipulated the parents and tried to manipulate her by avoiding the pre-practice coaching session. He has a thing or two to learn about me, she mused, grinning. She might not hit a home run every time she came up to bat, but her dogged persistence got her on base nine times out of ten. If necessary, she'd hound him into being prepared to coach.

She shifted the bag to ease its weight on her collarbone. Too bad she hadn't asked big, brawny Bubba to carry it. There was no doubt in her mind that he'd consider cleaning up and carrying the bag as part of "women's work." Next time, she promised herself as she staggered, next time she'd have the kids clean up after themselves and *order* Bubba to lug the equipment to her car.

"Hey, Joyce! How'd it go?"

24

Joyce straightened her stooped shoulders when she recognized the voice of the President of the Clear Lake Little League. "Hi, Cliff. Just let me get rid of this, okay?"

"Need some help?"

"No, thanks. I've got everything under control."

She balanced the canvas bag while she unhooked her keys from the loop on her shorts. Unlocking the sliding door of her custom van, she yanked it open, then dumped the bag on the carpet.

"We really appreciate your managing a team." Cliff removed his baseball cap and wiped his brow with his forearm. "We were desperate. I'd called everybody I knew when my wife suggested you."

Joyce grimaced, sliding the van door shut. Now she knew how Jim Carleton felt when Bubba pounded him between the shoulder blades. A bit more kindness from Bubba or Cliff and she'd be driven to her knees.

"I wondered how you'd come up with my name." Slowly turning, she forced herself to smile.

"Tammy raved about you. She says you're the best physical education teacher in the Houston area." Cliff plopped his cap back on his receding hairline. "Says your gymnastic teams are always winning medals."

He's laying it on thick, Joyce thought. Her

smile reached her eyes. She wondered what kind of favor he was going to ask her this time. Her natural tendency to be direct strained against the boundaries of being tactful.

"Well, uh," Cliff shifted from foot to foot uncomfortably. "Guess you've met the boys' parents?"

"Bubba Hawkins in particular?"

Defensively, Cliff said, "Now I know Bubba can be a blowhard, but deep down he's only got his son's best interests at heart."

Joyce clenched her teeth to keep a mildly dirty word from escaping.

"I don't suppose Bubba volunteered, uh, to be part of the, uh—"

"He's one of the coaches," Joyce said, completing Cliff's question. Why let Cliff suffer? Even the president of the league couldn't determine what parent went with each child. "I'll manage. Ben Williams's niece volunteered him as the other coach."

"Ben Williams? Good man from what I hear, but I'm surprised he has the free time."

"Did you call him?"

"I couldn't reach him."

"I will." The prospect of having Bubba as the only member of her coaching staff made Joyce determined to contact Ben Williams.

"Is there any equipment you need?"

"Everything checked out."

"Good." Cliff pointed toward the small, two-story building behind the catcher's screen. "The stuff to line the bases is under the scorekeepers' box. Home team is responsible for the field. Once a month the field manager drafts parents to help cut the grass." He handed her a stack of mimeographed sheets. "Scheduled games. Let's hope there aren't any rain out. Offhand, I can't think of anything else. You let me know if Ben Williams can't help, otherwise, I'll be seeing you opening day. Thanks again, Joyce."

"My pleasure."

Joyce watched Cliff hustle over to another team manager, remove his cap, wipe his brow, and begin his spiel. Whew! Few people realized how much work took place before the first game. She certainly hadn't.

Half an hour later, Joyce sat down at the dinette table in her condominium with a tall glass of iced tea and dialed Stacy's home number.

"Williams residence," Stacy answered.

"Hi, Stacy. This is Joyce MacIntyre. Is your uncle home?"

"UNCLE BEN! IT'S FOR YOU! IT'S MS. MACINTYRE!"

Joyce held the phone away from her ear until she was certain Stacy had finished. "Stacy? Did you say anything about coaching to him?"

"I told him how neat our manager is," Stacy replied, avoiding the question.

"Stacy."

"I told him about you catching a ball bare-

27

handed. Wowie! Your hand must be tough. Uncle Ben was impressed."

"Stacy!"

"And I told him how pretty your hair is. Mine used to be blond like yours, but . . ." her voice dropped to a whisper, ". . . you're going to have to convince him to coach." Her voice returned to a normal level; her tone changed from friendliness to stark politeness. "Nice talking to you, Ms. MacIntyre."

Joyce heard the receiver exchanging hands.

"Thanks, honey. You go finish your math homework."

The low, husky timbre of his voice splashed goosebumps across her arms. Salesman? Advertising? she thought, guessing what he did for a living. Whatever he sold, she'd bet there were a lot of women buying it.

"Bossy, bossy, bossy. You're always bossing me around," she heard Stacy shout from the background, getting the final word as she ran from the room.

"Yes, Ms. MacIntyre. What can I do for you?"

Leading question, Mr. Williams. At the moment, all she wanted to do was lean back, prop her feet up, and listen to anything the man had to say. Joyce capped her errant thoughts as quickly as a fielder caps a grounder.

"Help coach the Astros," she answered, her tongue dry and thick. She sipped her iced tea, waiting for a response.

28

"By any chance, did my niece volunteer my services?"

"Should she have?" Joyce countered.

"Uh-oh, she's worked her magic on you." His soft chuckle made her palms damp. "You don't want to get her in trouble, right?"

"Considering Stacy's family situation, I can understand why she wants you to coach."

"Ah, you couldn't resist those big, blue eyes and her sad little voice."

"Wait a minute, Mr. Williams. Stacy didn't do a number on me."

"The orphan story didn't get to you?"

Joyce heard a mixture of amusement and disbelief behind his question. "Maybe. A little," she finally admitted.

"Let me assure you, Ms. MacIntyre, Stacy wants for very little."

Smiling, taking advantage of an opportunity to pitch him a curve, Joyce retorted, "Then since your coaching is so important to her, I'm certain you won't refuse. Right?"

"Wrong."

Taking a deep breath, she repeated, "Wrong?"

"Ms. MacIntyre—"

"Joyce." She inserted her first name to keep him from verbalizing his refusal. She had a sneaking suspicion that once he'd refused, he wouldn't change his mind. "Not every child wants their guardian to be at every practice. She's going to be the star of the team. I'd hate for you to miss a rare opportunity because you're too . . ."

"Busy. Exactly. My first responsibility to Stacy is financial."

"Men!" Joyce scoffed lightheartedly. "You all think you'll miss a rung in that success ladder if you take the time to coach a kids' baseball team. It's little wonder that teenagers get into trouble to get their parents' attention."

"You're an authority on raising children? How many children do you have?"

"Two hundred and twenty-seven, not counting the gymnastic kids," she glibly answered. "That enough?"

Ben laughed.

Home run. Score one for the schoolteacher! The sheer delight she heard in his laughter raised her temperature. Joyce fanned her heated face with her hand. Her pulse throbbed raggedly. Attracted to his voice, she began to wonder how he looked. Tall? Short? Thin? Pudgy? She shrugged. Long ago she'd learned from a muscle-bound college football player that looks didn't mean a damned thing. Ben's charming laughter intrigued her.

Joyce MacIntyre hadn't been charmed or intrigued in a long, long time.

More than ever, Joyce hoped he'd reconsider joining the coaching staff.

"Stacy said you look like Marilyn Monroe and catch balls like Wonder Woman deflecting bullets from her wrists. Interesting combination."

30

"She says you're bossy. You believe half of what she tells you at home, and I'll believe half of what she tells me at baseball practice," Joyce bargained. "Or better yet, find out for yourself by agreeing to coach."

"It's hard to turn down Little Orphan Annie and Wonder Woman. You're very persuasive."

Determined, Joyce silently corrected, seizing his tentative agreement and translating it into a firm commitment. "Terrific. I'll mail you a packet of information and look forward to seeing you Wednesday night for a pre-practice meeting. Thanks. 'Bye."

"Wait!"

Joyce disconnected the line, grinning from ear to ear. "That was a lousy trick," she gloated. Not feeling the least bit repentant, she took the phone off the hook.

CHAPTER TWO

Joyce picked up the phone and dialed Bubba Hawkins's number for the tenth time in two days. Busy! she blasted. Taking the phone off the hook must be contagious. Yesterday, she'd considered driving by his house, but decided she didn't want to see him any sooner than necessary.

She checked her watch. "In less than ten minutes Ben Williams will be here. Tomorrow, we practice."

Pacing between the phone and the front door, she glanced at herself in the mirror. She'd wanted to dress in blue shorts and the official team T-shirt that had MANAGER in bold letters across the back. There was nothing quite like having two-inch letters to establish who was boss. Unfortunately, the shipment of manager's shirts had been delayed.

Strike one.

She'd considered wearing one of the award-emblazoned leotards she'd been presented with at the last gymnastic meet. Too ostentatious, too revealing, she'd decided.

Two strikes.

Finally, she'd chosen a one-piece jumpsuit made of a Hawaiian cotton print. She turned sideways, then to the back. Her straight, ash-blond hair swished provocatively below her waist. Her usual ponytail might have been better. Remembering how Bubba had called her "girl" was the reason behind wearing it down. Ponytails were practical, but accentuated her youthful appearance. She doubted Bubba Hawkins would attend the meeting, but she'd have given herself a buzz haircut rather than hit a foul ball.

"I'm thinking in baseball terminology," she caught herself. "So? The Spanish teacher says a person doesn't really know a foreign language until they start thinking in it." She smiled. Joyce knew baseball inside and out. For the next two months she'd be eating, drinking, and sleeping baseball. And loving it!

Joyce strode into the kitchen and picked up the phone. "One more time, Bubba!"

The busy signal droned in her ear; the doorbell rang. Joyce slammed down the receiver, dashed to the door, and opened it wide.

Her eyes rounded as her dark pupils snapped a mental picture of Ben Williams lounging against the porch railing, a lopsided smile greeting her, black onyx eyes twinkling, with an aluminum bat making lazy circles in the sky.

A grand slam with the bases loaded!

"Hi, I'm Stacy's uncle. Ben Williams."

"Oh! Of course, I've been expecting you. I'm Joyce MacIntyre."

Over the years Joyce had met a wide variety of musclebound men, but few compared favorably with Ben Williams. Her eyes were drawn to the wide navy blue stripe across his chest which accentuated the breadth of his chest and complemented his pale blue shirt. Cotton navy shorts matched the stripe. White socks and tennis shoes emphasized his dark tan.

"You're supposed to invite me in," he coached, closing the distance between them. Ben spread his arms wide. "It's a beautiful evening. Maybe you planned on holding the meeting on the porch?"

Joyce glanced toward the old-fashioned wooden swing that hung from the porch rafters. She shook her head, and said wistfully, "I'm afraid the swing won't hold the weight of all three of us. Please, come in."

"Three of us?"

"Umm. Bubba Hawkins is the other coach." She ushered him into the living room. "Do you know him?"

"Not to my recollection."

"Can I get you something to drink? Coffee? Tea?" *Me?*

"Nothing, thanks. Stacy and I just polished off a pitcher of Mrs. Shane's fresh lemonade." Ben

34

propped the bat against the end table and sat in the center of the sofa. In a single sweep, he glanced around the room. Far more slowly, his eyes flicker over Joyce. "Nice. Beautifully decorated."

Knees weak, tongue-tied, Joyce crossed the room with the same precise steps she used when preparing to mount a balancing beam. With a perfect stranger sitting on the sofa, she usually chose to seat herself in the nearby wing chair. She eased herself onto the edge of the cushion to the left of Ben. To avoid sitting on her hair, she looped it over her right shoulder.

Abruptly Joyce was confronted with a problem: what am I going to do with my hands? *Brush the windblown lock of hair off his brow,* her libido commanded. Her fingers balled, not obeying the command. *Stroke his strong jaw line and see if it's as smooth as it looks. Investigate the slight V of his shirt . . .* She felt like slapping her own face to get her thoughts within the boundaries of propriety. What was she going to do with them? Suspended in the air, she fanned her face. "Hot, isn't it?"

Ben leaned back, making himself comfortable. "Spring weather in Texas tends to be warm."

While he spoke, Joyce fretted. She could put her hands on her lap, but her knees were scant inches from his. No pockets. Sit on them? Wring them? Spying the stack of Little League schedules, she picked them up, dropped one in Ben's lap, balanced the stack on her knees, and laced her fingers together on top of them.

"What kind of experience do you have?" she asked, futilely making an effort to give some semblance of being an adult able to cope with any situation while she gathered her wits. Ben's grin spread. For heaven's sake, her question sounded like something a madam would ask a masseur. "Coaching," she clarified. "Coaching experience."

Ben covered his mouth with one crooked finger to keep from chuckling. Joyce MacIntyre was absolutely adorable. He'd expected a musclebound female jock. The pink tinge slowly climbing from her neck to her high cheekbones assured Ben that she was extremely feminine, sexy in a wholesome way.

"I've played for years," he replied, with a hint of mischief, "almost every position. What position do you like best?"

The husky, low pitch of his voice made Joyce want to lean closer. The connotation she put on his reply was way out in left field. Or was it? His dark eyes sparkled with a devilish twinkle. Was he in telepathic communication with her libido?

"Umpire," she quipped. His eyebrow arched. "They call all the plays."

"Foul and fair?"

Joyce knew he'd baited a verbal trap. She felt herself falling. "Umm," she responded noncommittally.

"Call this play, Ump. My niece is up to bat. The ball lobs across the plate. Outside."

"Easy. Ball one."

Bending at the waist, Ben leaned with his elbows on his knees. "Stacy flashes you a smile."

He grinned.

Joyce melted.

"Stacy's glove touches the catcher's mitt." His hand crossed to lightly touch her knee.

"Warning," Joyce squeaked.

"Stacy steps out of the batter's box. Her lips droop forlornly."

"Batter up!"

His hand hadn't moved. She wanted to brush it aside, but her fingers remained locked together, unresponsive to her directive.

"Stacy's back in the box, hunched over the plate. The ball is pitched."

"Yes?"

"Well?"

"You didn't tell me if it was in the strike zone."

Ben laughed. "Now you know how I felt when you hung up the other night. The pitch was thrown, but before I could decided if it was in the strike zone or not, you hung up. Stacy definitely threw a wild pitch. I've warned her time and time again not to volunteer me for every activity she participates in."

"Parental, or in your case, guardian involvement in student activities is a display of love."

"What textbook did that come out of?"

Joyce had the good grace to blush. "Child Psychology 101."

"Now you're playing fair," he complimented, patting her knee. "Would you consider it 'fair' for me to be volunteered as second grade room mother? In charge of the bakery booth at the school carnival?" Joyce chuckled and shook her head. "How about assistant instructor to the baton twirlers? Fair?"

"Foul," she called, holding her ribs and leaning back in the corner of the sofa.

"Don't forget. Stacy is forlorn. If I refuse, I'm a 'cussed sidewinder' in her book."

Joyce laughed harder. She tried to picture Ben in a twirler's costume, with tights and a tall hat, blowing a whistle, but her vivid imagination couldn't stretch that far.

"Ready to call the play on the coup de grace? She signed me up for a kissing booth? I don't claim to have virgin lips, but I certainly—quit laughing. Saying 'no' to Stacy has become serious business."

Blinking to keep the tears of laughter back, she tried to straighten up, but failed.

"And last, but not least, Stacy volunteered me to coach baseball."

"You won't have to wear a teensy-weensy skirt," Joyce promised.

"Thanks a heap."

"Or kiss . . ." Her mouth parched. She swallowed. The tip of her tongue wet the bow of her lower lip. ". . . the players."

"You left out the umpire."

"High school boys umpire the games."

"Coaching staff?"

He was close. Very close. Close enough for Joyce to smell his woodsy aftershave. Was that his breathing she heard? Hers? Uncertain, she inhaled deeply. Damn, it was hers!

"Bubba isn't your type."

"The manager?"

His eyes skated across the faint freckles on the bridge of her nose. What would it be like to kiss him? she wondered. Joyce bit the inside of her lip to keep from blurting, "Yes!"

"No." She tapped the papers on lap. "Not required."

Ben covered her hand. "You're sure?"

Sure? At this second, she wasn't sure about anything other than the depth of his eyes, the breadth of his shoulders, the taut muscles of his thighs. She needed him to help coach. She had to stifle the other needs rampantly running through her.

"Positive."

"Umm. I think I'd like that glass of ice water you offered earlier."

Joyce wriggled from his grasp, scrambled to her feet. "Why don't you skim through the rulebook while I'm getting your drink," she suggested, hoping he'd find a loophole about kissing the manager.

After she'd filled a glass with ice, she ran the tap water over her wrists. Some manager she'd turned out to be. Ben was in her house for five minutes and they were flirting instead of planning team strategy. She was the manager but his masculinity had made her extremely aware of her vulnerable femininity.

"Friendly persuasion?" she muttered, drying her hands. "Far more effective than being bossy, but equally subversive. Bubba Hawkins isn't going to manage this team, and neither is Ben Williams."

"Did you call me?"

Joyce inwardly jumped. Ben had followed her into the kitchen.

"I'm terrible about remembering names," she fibbed. "I say names out loud to help me remember." She glanced over her shoulder and saw that he didn't believe a word she'd said. She wasn't about to admit she'd been in the kitchen giving herself a pep talk. Keeping her eyes on the wallpaper above his head, adding starch to her tone of voice, she said, "Looks like Bubba isn't coming. Bring the rulebook and papers in here. We'll finish up our business at the kitchen table."

Ben raised his hands, holding the items she'd mentioned. "I brought them with me."

Damn! He's one step ahead of me again. Her eyes dropped to his powerful hands. When she

40

saw only one book, one set of schedules, she smiled. She couldn't let him outmaneuver her. She gestured for Ben to be seated, saying, "I'll get my own book. I already have it marked."

"Would you mind getting me a highlight pen if you don't want to share the same book."

"The pens are in the pencil holder behind you." *Get it yourself.* Giving an order that countermanded his polite command pleased her. She could be subtle, too. Stacy had warned her about her uncle being bossy. No man was going to boss Joyce MacIntyre around.

She gathered her materials from the living room and sat down across the table from Ben. She flipped the booklet open. "Page one, section six. Watches, rings, etc., are forbidden."

For the next half hour, they went over the rules. Ben pointed out the changes that had been made since he'd played.

"It's almost like a whole new ballgame," Ben grumbled. "Some of the rules seem pretty silly to me. Like the one about the coaches touching the players."

Joyce closed the final page of her booklet. "Exuberant coaches have been known to give their players a push to get them started to the next base. You haven't any idea how wild some of these parents can be at Little League sporting events."

Their eyes caught and held. She ducked her head. Whatever kind of game he was playing, she was going to be the one making the rules. She wouldn't let a pair of dazzling eyes, or a sexy voice, or a great set of shoulders distract her from her goal of managing a victorious team.

"It's time for me to go," Ben said, pushing his chair back.

"Not yet. We haven't divided the players into squads."

"Believe me, Joyce, it is time to leave it." He got to his feet, picked up his papers. "I'll divide the team into squads."

"That's my job, my responsibility," she protested. "I wanted input from you and Bubba as to your coaching strengths and weaknesses. I'll decide who's going to pitch. Who's coaching first base. Who's . . . in . . . charge . . . of . . . running!"

Ben strode toward the front door muttering indistinctly. Following in his footsteps, she couldn't decipher what he was saying. Ben suddenly stopped; Joyce plowed into his backside. He pivoted and caught her by the shoulders.

His voice rang with authority. "I'll coach the kids on how to run the bases."

Joyce tilted her head upward and grinned. Behind his façade of wicked, devilish glances, he had felt the chemical attraction between them. She hadn't been alone in the ballpark.

"You're good at running, aren't you?"

"Practice makes perfect."

Encouraged by his admission, she bluntly, cou-

42

rageously asked, "What are you running away from?"

"A sexy-as-hell, teacher–team manager, who's been calling the plays all night." His hands slid from her shoulders to her elbows, and back up again.

He'd driven her crazy earlier in the evening with his tantalizing innuendos. Turnabout was fair play. "Afraid of the ball?" she boldly tormented, raising on tiptoes.

She'd pushed too hard not to expect repercussions. Ben threaded his fingers into the silky length of her hair, tilting her head until their lips met. His lips were soft, gentle, rocking back and forth, tormenting her without words, remaining closed.

"Still scared?" she whispered when their lips parted. His lips hovered over hers as though making a momentous decision.

Sizzling seconds later, he answered, "Petrified. Worse than the first time I stepped into the batter's box with all my friends and neighbors watching."

Joyce could barely hear him.

"I'm scared to death of winding up like my brother did."

"Stacy's dad? Are you talking about his death?"

"No. His death was a tragedy. He and his wife were casualties of a terrorist bombing of a foreign airport."

"Then what do you mean?" Joyce probed.

Ben continued. "Stacy's mom led my brother around by a ring in his nose. I don't like bossy women, Joyce MacIntyre. They're more trouble than they're worth. When I'm attracted to one" —he turned and quickly moved through the door —"I run."

Before she could grab him by the shirt front, he was gone.

"Quitter!" she yelled from the porch at his retreating back.

Ben shot her a dirty look as he opened his car door. "Nobody has ever called me a quitter. You make a list of what has to be done, and I'll do it."

"Now who's being bossy! I'll make a list *if I feel like it!*"

Joyce shut the door with more force than necessary. She hated dictatorial men as much as he hated bossy women. He wasn't going to tell her what to do!

She marched into the living room and slumped into a chair. Arms folded across her chest, she glared at the cushion where Ben Williams had been seated. She caught sight of Stacy's bat. A cheeky grin replaced her scowl.

Ben would be back, like it or not. Stacy would make him retrieve her belongings. Her bat was probably as important to her as her worn glove.

There must have been some reason for Ben bringing it to her house. She picked it up. Longer than most, lighter, she assessed. Would it meet the league's regulation size and weight guidelines? She'd have to check that out with Cliff James. There was no doubt in her mind that the league had a rule about size and weight. They had a rule for everything!

She stored the bat in the front closet, then walked into the kitchen. Ben had taken his packet of information. Hers lay on the table.

So he wants a list, does he? What I ought to do is make a list of every dirty job that has to be done and assign him to it. And seal it with a wild, red lipstick kiss.

She picked up a pencil, and hastily scribbled: *Coach outfielders.*

Kids hated playing in the outfield where there was little or no action. Working with disgruntled players who half-listened to instruction while watching the infield practice was a difficult task. All twelve players wanted to be pitcher, catcher, first baseman, or shortstop. The remaining positions lacked peer status and glory. Ben would have a tough time holding their attention.

Clean under bleachers before and after each game.

That's a dandy, Joyce mused. Mothers, especially meticulous housekeepers at home, became full-fledged slobs while they watched their little darlings play ball. Candy wrappers, paper cups, cheesy remains of nachos fluttered to the ground. Bubble gum stuck to the bottom of the seats, like malevolent snipers in trees, waited until the unsuspecting prey was close then, zap, it seemed to grab hold of the nearest lock of hair. Joyce had used more than one tray of ice removing Bubble-Yummy from her hair.

Weed and mow field.

Another time-consuming, thankless job. The Little League budget wouldn't stretch far enough to hire ground maintenance people.

Line field.

The home team was responsible for putting the three-inch strips of lime on the field to mark the boundaries. Another thankless job requiring the person in charge to arrive half an hour early for the game.

Fill potholes in baseball diamond. Water field.

With what? Sand wasn't provided. Neither were hoses and sprinklers. The person this job was relegated to had to provide his or her own resources.

Carry equipment.

Ben would have an opportunity to use those shoulder muscles of his. Plus, he'd have the side benefit of having to stick around after the game to collect the bases. More time well spent.

Joyce glanced over the list, supremely satisfied.

"He thinks his job, whatever it is, keeps him too busy to coach?" she mused a bit spitefully. "I'll have so damn much for him to do, he'll have to quit working!"

CHAPTER THREE

At ten to five on Thursday afternoon, Joyce lugged the equipment bag toward the practice field. Stacy, Bobby, and Ricky were tossing a ball back and forth. Ricky invariably missed catching it; his inaccuracy throwing matched his catching skills.

"Hey, Astros, how about some help?" Joyce dumped the canvas bag on the ground beside the cyclone-fenced backstop. "Stacy, you and Ricky put the bases around, and Bobby, you put the batting helmets on the sidelines with the bats."

Stacy and Ricky haggled over the exact placement of the base bags. Ricky wanted them as close to home plate as possible. Joyce grinned at Stacy's insistence. She was the only girl on the team, but she wasn't going to let anyone boss her around.

"A girl after my own heart," Joyce muttered to herself.

Turning toward the side street she saw Jacob's mother, Lucille, ·wave from her car as she dropped off five members of the team, and right behind them, she spotted Mickey half-running, half-walking to keep up with Ben Williams's long strides.

Joyce wiped her brow with a small towel she kept tucked in the front of her shorts. Blame it on the sun, she tried to convince herself, knowing that the late-afternoon sun had little to do with her heart pounding against her rib cage.

Ben's faded cut-off jeans and red T-shirt molded his athletic frame to perfection. She caught glimpses of his smile as he talked to Mickey. A breeze blowing off Galveston Bay whipped his dark hair. Her fingers positively itched to replace his hand as it riffled his forelock back into place.

Think about baseball, she silently chided her wayward mind.

Joyce removed the clipboard from beneath her arm, giving the coaches' assignment a quick once-over. Her innate sense of fairness had overruled her momentary bout of spite. She'd divided the irksome chores between the two coaches and herself.

She'd also divided the team into three squads of four players. Each coach would start the practice by throwing a few grounders and pop flys to warm up the players. Ben and Bubba were to pay attention to which players they felt had potential to be infield players.

The second half of the practice, she'd halved

48

the team. Six of them would have infield practice with her. The other six would have batting practice with Ben and Bubba. During a game, the outfielders would rotate into the game on alternate innings. Every child, according to Little League rules, played a minimum of two innings. Joyce knew the players relegated to the outfield would be somewhat disappointed. Batting practice, the kids' favorite activity, would make up for not being chosen for a key infield position.

"Hi, Joyce."

Ben's casual greeting triggered her memory. She'd forgotten how his low husky voice sent goosebumps shivering up her spine, and tingling downward to the backs of her knees.

"Hi, Ben." Her voice sounded breathy as though she'd been running laps around the bases. Clearing her throat, she handed Ben his assignment sheets. She watched his dark eyes narrow as he scanned the sheets. Long, curly eyelashes that an actor would have killed for cast shadows beneath his eyes. His brow furrowed in concentration. She realized she'd been holding her breath, waiting for his approval when a near-sigh passed through her lips.

Ben held the papers loosely between his fingers at her chest level. It wasn't intention, he fibbed to himself when his eyes strayed to the shallow vee of her pink and blue plaid blouse. A wry smile curved his lips as his eyes dropped. Joyce MacIntyre had the best legs of any manager in the league.

He pulled a folded piece of notebook paper from his front pocket, compared it with her list of extra duties, and grinned as he handed it to her.

Making a quick comparison herself, she found the duties she'd assigned and the duties he'd volunteered for were identical. Mixed emotions struggled for supremacy. On the one hand, she appreciated his willingness to do more than his share; but on the other hand, she was the person responsible for assigning duties. He'd outsmarted her by volunteering. Venting her spleen would make her appear churlish. Saying nothing gave him the upper hand as to who was managing the team.

"Great minds think alike?" Ben asked, giving both of them credit for knowing what chores needed to be done. The wee pout of her lips was so damned kissable. He'd deliberately planned to stay one step ahead of her, knowing she was a "take charge" woman, knowing how she'd react. But now, with his pulse beating a wild tattoo, he wished he'd shredded his list into confetti.

"Who's going to pitch during batting practice?" he asked, slowly raising his eyes to meet hers. Against his will, he felt his body tighten. Momentarily he forgot his dislike for overorganized women shoving pages of lists into his hands. Two steps, and twelve pairs of eyes avidly watching the grownups, separated him from tossing her clipboard aside and kissing her until she was too breathless to berate him for figuratively stepping on her bossy toes.

"B-B-Bubba," Joyce sputtered, "you, me." She stepped backward, resisting the magnetic pull of his eyes, hating how her tongue seemed to be tied in an awkward knot.

"Three pitchers? Won't it get a mite crowded on the pitcher's mound?" Ben teased, pleased to find her equally flustered.

Joyce answered the dictates of her body first. "Yes!" Realizing he was joking, she babbled, "One pitcher at a time. We'll decide which one of the three of us the kids are mostly likely to get hits off of."

"It's hard for me to adjust to the idea of pitching to my own team. Usually the opponents' team has a player on the pitcher's mound."

"Five-pitch baseball is designed to give the young players a feeling of success," Joyce explained needlessly.

Although they gave the appearance of casually discussing the rules, an undercurrent of electricity passed back and forth between them. What their mouths said was insignificant compared to what their eyes communicated.

"Fun and games rather than serious competition?" Ben quizzed.

She shook her head, aware of his eyes watching the long swath of hair she'd pulled through the opening in the back of her baseball cap. "The

51

game gets serious by the end of the season. There won't be a parent in the stands who doesn't want to see their team take first place. It's our job to make certain the kids aren't pressured. We want it to be fun, so they'll play again next year."

Joyce completed the canned spiel she'd planned on giving Bubba. Intuitively, she knew Ben wouldn't allow Stacy to participate in a sport hell-bent on winning. She'd talked to avoid touching him. A verbal barrier was the only thing keeping her from throwing the lists aside and twining her arms around his broad shoulders. She broke eye contact, to rein in her impulsive desires.

"Where's Bubba?" She turned and looked toward the street. "We need to get started."

Her head snapped back toward Ben when she heard, "Umm-yes. We do *need* to get on with it."

It? It! His lazy smile and bright eyes assured her baseball practice was not what he was talking about. Right in front of her Little League team, she was falling prey to his seductive eyes.

Oh no, Joyce thought, mentally adding starch to her manager's uniform. She was here for fun and games with the kids. Mr. Ben Williams would have to find another playmate. She wouldn't allow herself to be distracted.

"Let's warm up," she called, feeling decidedly hot already.

Within minutes, she had five kids lined across from Ben and six across from herself. "Throw to the chest." She thudded her front with the flat of her hand. "Right here."

"Ya'll can't miss 'em," Bubba said, pounding Sonny's shoulders knowingly in a man-to-man slap.

Joyce tossed the ball to Rick. While he was chasing it, she wheeled around to Bubba. "You're late, Bubba. We'll have kids straggling in late to practice if the coaches can't get here on time."

Ignoring her, Bubba picked up a bat and said, "Hey, who wants to practice batting with Sonny and me?"

"Hold it!" Joyce raised her hands to stop the fielders from making a mad dash toward the batting helmets. "We're warming up first. You missed the coaches' meeting. You'll have to read the top sheet on the clipboard for your coaching assignment."

"Assignment?" Bubba thumped Sonny's shoulders. Sonny winced, then ran to the line of fielders. "Where do ya think we are, Ms. MacIntyre? In the classroom? I'm here to teach these here youngsters how to score runs. That's how games are won."

Ben stepped between Joyce and Bubba. "Bubba, I'm Ben Williams," he said, introducing himself, thrusting his hand forward to be shaken. "Since we've started without you, let's follow the guidelines for today's practice."

"Ya ain't gonna let no little woman tell us men what to do, are ya?" Bubba's meaty hand clasped

Ben's in a bone-grinding shake. His eyes narrowed as Ben returned an equal amount of pressure. With a laugh, he clapped Ben on the shoulders. "We men gotta stick together."

"Don't let him get to you," Ben cautioned Joyce in quiet tones. "He's the kind of guy who'd love to see you stomp your feet and bawl."

Joyce gave Ben a weak grin. "Thanks, but I've dealt with Bubba's brand of chivalry-coated machismo all my life. I'll spit in his eye before he sees me cry."

Catching the ball Bubba lobbed at her, she was tempted to check his reflexes by hurling it back at sixty to seventy miles an hour. Biting the inside of her lip, she threw a hard grounder to Stacy. "Cap it," she called as Stacy scooped up the ball.

She caught a glimpse of the ball Sonny whizzed to his father. Barehanded, Bubba caught the ball, then shook his fingers as though his fingernails had caught on fire. Sonny beamed his father an innocent smile.

Rebellion on the home front, Joyce pondered. Sonny had to live with his overbearing father. The kid had certainly been merciless regarding his father's unprotected hands.

"Thattaboy," Bubba hooted. "Sting my hands. We ain't gonna have sissies with shirts on their backs sayin' they're studs." Bubba shot Joyce and Stacy a dirty look. "Well, maybe one or two sissies," he corrected with macho sarcasm.

Joyce considered the source of the denigrating

remark, shrugged it off, and lobbed a pop fly–type ball toward Mickey. "Keep your eye on the ball," she instructed, as much for herself as for the child. "Get under it. Catch it. Cap it. Good catch. Now, when you throw the ball, step with your left foot, then use your whole arm to throw as you step with your right foot. Follow through. Keep your hand pointed at me for a second after you've thrown the ball. Beautiful," she said when the ball landed squarely in the pocket of her glove.

"Okay, Ricky. Let's see you do the same."

Encouragement, praise, and challenge. Those were positive elements of coaching Bubba missed. Yelling and berating a child would result in shaking the player's confidence. Eventually the child would learn to hate the sport and the coach. Joyce wouldn't allow that to happen. At the next coaches' meeting she'd have some coaching tips for Bubba.

Minutes later, she called an end to fielding practice. After consulting with Ben and Bubba, they decided which players were most likely to consistently catch the ball and assigned them to bases. Sonny played first; Stacy played shortstop; Mickey played second; Bobby on third. To give Jacob additional practice catching, she chose him as catcher. According to Little League rules, a batter couldn't steal a base if the catcher dropped the ball.

Joyce stood on home base and pretended to be

the batter. Teamwork was essential. The kids had to know where to throw the ball when it came to them.

Gradually, Joyce coached the basemen from making split-second, simple decisions to decisions with complex alternatives.

"Man on first," Joyce called to the infielders. "Stacy, where are you going to throw it?"

"To second," Stacy shouted. "Then Mickey's going to throw it to first for a double play."

"What if it's a pop fly and you catch it?" Joyce asked, complicating the fielding.

"The batter's out. I throw it to second. Mickey catches it and tags the runner for two outs!"

"Here it comes." Joyce threw a grounder. Stacy caught it, lobbed it to second. Mickey fumbled it. Before the kids could say anything, Joyce said, "That's okay, Mickey. You tried. Throw it to first." Mickey made up for dropping the ball by making a perfect throw to first. "Sonny, take it easy and throw it to Jacob. Teamwork . . . remember . . . it's teamwork that makes a player valuable."

Sonny grinned.

She half-expected Sonny to throw the ball hard, but was pleasantly surprised to find him considerate of his less capable teammate.

"Here ya go, Jacob."

Sonny lobbed the ball to home plate. Jacob missed it, but promised, "I'll get the next one."

Glancing downfield, Joyce saw Bubba on the

mound pitching. He threw a hard, fast ball, straight across the strike zone. Darn it, Bubba, you know those kids don't have a prayer of hitting a ball they can barely see. Slow it down.

Ben, squatting behind the plate, caught the ball and threw it to Bubba. He said something Joyce couldn't hear. Laughing at Ben's comment, Bubba fired another pitch: same speed, same accuracy.

"Slow it down!" she heard Ben yell. "These kids . . ." His voice failed to carry the remainder of his instructions across the field for Joyce to hear.

Bubba lobbed the ball. From where Joyce stood, she knew it would take a physics major to determine the precise moment when to swing. The batter swung and missed. Frustrated, the child pounded the plate with the tip of the aluminum bat.

"That's three strikes," Bubba gloated.

Ben patted the deflated child on the shoulders, encouraging him.

Joyce called another play to the infielders. She wanted to give Bubba the sharp edge of her tongue. Nothing irked her more than seeing a grown man belittle a budding athlete.

Bubba returned to his speed ball. Ben stood, hands on his hips, then marched out to the pitcher's mound. Joyce would have given a month's paycheck to have a listening device on the ball in Ben's glove. She watched Ben's hand swat Bubba's rear end. She grinned when Bubba took the catcher's mask and pulled it over his face.

She'd previously decided not to be the team's pitcher. Her team would get plenty of flak because they had a woman manager without her flaunting her position by being pitcher. Coaching from the first base line was by far more preferable.

"Okay, team. Let's get in some batting practice. First one to the other end of the field is lead batter."

With a loud "Whoopee," all six kids took off lickety-split. Sonny had a head start. Stacy, like a graceful gazelle, passed him halfway down the field. Joyce watched Bubba's face twist distastefully as his son came in second. He didn't physically cuff the boy, but the withering glare he gave Sonny left no doubt as to how he felt about letting a girl win the race.

"Uncle Ben left my lucky bat at your house," Stacy said, scowling at her guardian. "Did you bring it?"

"It's with the league bats by the fence," Joyce replied.

Once Stacy had her lucky bat and Joyce had her hand on the runner's shoulder, safely away from the swing of the bat, Ben pitched the ball.

"High and outside," Bubba called. "C'mon, coach, get 'em across the plate. The parents will eat you alive if you walk their kid."

"You can do it, Uncle Ben," Stacy encouraged,

58

taking a practice swing that came within inches of the catcher's mask.

His second pitch crossed Stacy at the waist; she swung and made contact. The ball skittered between second and third.

Stacy jumped up and down as the runner tagged first base and headed for second. "Faster, you can make it!"

"Slide," Bubba bellowed, tossing off his mask. "Slide!"

The runner made second base . . . on his feet.

"Didn't ya hear Miz Joyce say not to slide," Sonny said, openly chastising his father.

"Watch yer lip, Sonny boy. I know what I'm doin'," Bubba huffed, squatting behind home plate.

Sonny slammed the helmet on his head. Stacy handed Sonny the bat, rolling her big blue eyes in sympathy for her new buddy.

"Use your bat, Sonny." Then to Ben, "Pitch it hard. My boy knows the harder they come in, the harder they go out. Step into the pitch. Don't let me see that bat touch your shoulder, boy, ya hear?"

Ben was caught in a dilemma. Should he follow the father's instructions, or throw Sonny the same kind of ball Stacy had hit? Deciding Bubba knew his kid better than he did, Ben sped up the pace. Sonny swung a fraction of a second too late.

"You missed an easy one, boy." Bubba glared up at his son and tossed the ball back to the pitcher's mound. "You fanned air like an old woman. Smack it!"

Joyce watched Sonny's face tighten. His hands gripped the bat until his knuckles were white. Pressure. Stress. Desire to please his father. Tight-lipped, the boy's face reflected his inner emotions.

As the next pitch nearly crossed the plate, Sonny pasted the ball with all his contained frustration. It soared as though hitting the ball had made it sprout wings.

"Thattaboy," Bubba cheered, suddenly the proud papa. "Home-run hitter!"

While the outfielder chased the ball, the runner ran the bases, and the kids boisterously cheered, Joyce and Ben's eyes met. Much as she hated Bubba's technique, she'd be a fool to argue with success. Sonny had hit a homer. In a real game, two runs would have scored.

Ben barely shook his head. Aren't you the one who said winning isn't everything? he silently questioned. You're the manager. Are you going to allow Bubba to bully the kids?

Joyce interpreted Ben's look and shuddered. The desire to win battled with her sense of fairness. She'd be flat out lying to deny wanting to win, but at what cost? That was the fine line Ben was drawing. How far was she willing to go in her quest to win? She'd readily admit to pushing herself to the breaking point while competing.

60

Would she push six- and eight-year-old children to their mental and physical endurance limits?

Joyce stepped to the batter's plate. "Good hit, Sonny. Who's next?"

By nonchalantly praising Sonny, she hoped she'd let the rest of the team know she wouldn't push for a passel of home-run hitters. "Keep your eye on the ball and do your best. Sonny showed you where the power is on the bat. Where'd he hit it?"

"On the tip end," Bobby volunteered.

"That's the way to learn, Bobby," she praised. "A full, level swing, with the ball hitting the bat on the tip end will get you a strong hit. You won't hit that magic spot every time. But, remember, no one," she turned to Bubba, "will criticize you unless you quit trying."

After each player had an opportunity to bat and run the bases, Joyce called an end to the practice. She passed the season's schedule to each child to take home to their parents. "Practice next—?"

"Tuesday!" the players piped.

"When?"

"Five o'clock."

"Sharp," Joyce added for Bubba's benefit. "Latecomers bat last."

Bubba nudged her arm. "I jest read your extra duty sheet. Ya expect *me* to pick up under the bleachers? That's woman's work." He ripped off the bottom part of the paper and wadded it in his

61

hand, belligerently letting it drop to the ground. "The parents drafted me to coach, not to play housewife."

Refraining from the urge to pick up the wad of paper and stuff it in Bubba's mouth, Joyce used her full powers of concentration to remain calm. Her mind churned, searching for a viable solution.

"Is it 'man's work' to handle the finances?" she asked with saccharine sweetness.

Bubba hiked up his pants. "I control the money in my house."

Joyce smiled. She had team mothers who disliked collecting money and a coach who disliked picking up litter. Time for a switch hitter. "Fine, Bubba. I'll let you be responsible for collecting the picture money, candy money, snow-cone money, pizza-party money, trophy money—"

"Now jest a minute, girlie. I'm too busy to . . ."

Ben, who'd played the role of impartial bystander, switched to devil's advocate. He couldn't allow Bubba to browbeat and intimidate Joyce. "You wouldn't want a mere woman to mismanage the money, would you? She might commingle the funds and bankrupt the league."

"I ain't no secretary neither," Bubba blustered, fingering his large belt buckle that proudly displayed the Lone Star emblem.

Joyce smiled. "Why don't you give this problem some thought between now and the first game?"

"Nothin' to think about. I ain't gonna pick up trash and I ain't gonna handle petty cash." Bubba stalked toward the parking lot where Sonny waited in his pickup truck. "And I ain't gonna git here by five o'clock!"

Covering her mouth to muffle a giggle, Joyce turned toward Ben. "Have you got a 'ain't gonna' list?"

Ben's respect for Joyce climbed a couple of notches. While Bubba was busy banging his chest, making he-man noises, she had coolly outwitted him. Confident Bubba would choose the less arduous task of cleaning under the bleachers rather than taking his valuable time to collect money, Ben grinned.

"No, ma'am," he replied. He hoisted the equipment bag to his shoulder. "Come on, Stacy. Mrs. Shane will have dinner waiting."

CHAPTER FOUR

Stacy sidled up to Ben and gave him a wide-eyed, innocent smile. "Mrs. Shane said I could bring company for dinner. We're having wienies and beans."

"Who'd you invite? Prissy from next door?" Ben inquired, shifting the canvas bag to his other shoulder.

Joyce lagged behind them making quick notations beside the players' names on her clipboard. At Tuesday's practice she wanted to shift Sonny to the pitcher's position. Although the coach did the actual pitching, a player stood beside the coach. With Stacy playing shortstop and Sonny playing pitcher, she'd have a tight infield.

Her eyes raised. "Talk about a tight infield," she murmured under her breath as she watched the play of Ben's shorts.

Stacy threw her glove high in the air, jumped, and caught it. She darted back to Joyce. "Guess what? I've invited you to dinner and Uncle Ben says you can come. Beans and wienies. Yum-yum! He said I'm not to pull any tricks."

Taken off stride by the unexpected invitation, Joyce stumbled on a tuft of grass. She regained her loss of balance and hesitated. "What kind of tricks is he talking about?"

"Oh, you know—poor-little-orphan-Stacy stuff. Uncle Ben is like an elephant. He doesn't remember the important stuff, but he always remembers tricks I pull to get what I want." She made a gruesome face. "Last week he threatened to spank my pa-toot just because I told a neighbor lady that he lets me stay up till midnight every night."

Joyce schooled her face to keep from smiling. One thing Stacy and her vivid imagination didn't need was encouragement. "Why in the world would you tell such a whopper?"

"To get the neighbor lady over to our house late at night to check—when I'm sound asleep and can't hear what's going on downstairs." Stacy gave Joyce a peculiar look and scoffed, "For a smart team manager, that wasn't a brilliant question. Uncle Ben is single, available, good-looking, and has lots of M-O-N-E-Y." Her voice lowered to a whisper as she confided, "I'm not supposed to even say the word M-O-N-E-Y, except with Uncle Ben."

Stacy's glib tongue rattled ninety to nothing saying anything that came into her mind. Joyce grinned at her lovable precociousness. Having heard Ben tell tales about the escapades she'd volunteered him for, she believed what his niece was telling her.

"Yeah. I told the PTA president, who's a divorcee, that Uncle Ben was so rich he lights his cigarettes with hundred-dollar bills. Man, he was really mad over that one. He said every gold digger in Texas would be camped outside our door if I kept spinning wild tales. The ol' sidewinder went around the house, shaking his head, muttering about gold diggers camping on our doorstep. Isn't that dumb? Even kindergarten kids know there aren't any gold mines in Texas. Stinky old oil wells, but no gold." She glanced toward her uncle, who was storing the bag in the back of a Cherokee. "Maybe he thought I buried his gold watch under the porch steps. Do you think that's what he meant?"

Joyce swallowed a chuckle. "Did you bury his gold watch under the front steps?"

"I don't remember. I was only four. Prissy from next door wanted to play treasure hunt. She borrowed some junky old jewelry from her mom's jewelry box. I don't have a mom with a jewelry box, so I kinda borrowed something from Uncle Ben's top dresser drawer."

"And?" Joyce prompted, caught up in Stacy's rambling story.

"Well, it's Uncle Ben's fault I couldn't find his watch. I was making a treasure map when he got all bossy about me eating dinner with him. Later, when I started digging up the backyard and told him about the buried treasure, he got beet red in the face 'cause I couldn't find the hole." Grinning, Stacy added, "Good thing I love the ol' sidewinder or I'd pack 'em up and ship him off to the zoo."

"He must love you, too," Joyce laughed.

"Yeah." Stacy turned and skipped backwards. "You're coming to dinner, aren't you?"

Joyce had a sneaking suspicion Stacy was trying to fix her up with her uncle. However, the other night Ben made his intentions crystal clear. He was attracted to her, but he was going to run like the devil to keep from being "led around by a ring in his nose."

"Let's see how receptive your uncle is to the idea first, okay?"

Stacy streaked to the Cherokee, shouting, "She says it's okay if you say okay."

"Stacy says you're the friend she invited to dinner." Ben shut the rear window with a sharp click. His niece had already scrambled into the backseat and was bouncing up and down. "Get in. After dinner I'll drive you back to pick up your car."

Bossy! Bossy! Joyce unhooked her key ring from her belt loop. She answered, "I'll follow."

Ben shrugged and got into the driver's seat and fastened his seat belt. Stacy climbed over to the empty front seat. She shot her uncle a baleful glare.

"Buckle up," he reminded.

"I'm going to let my hair grow long like Joyce's. Hers is beautiful."

"You're doing it again," Ben said, starting the engine.

"What?"

"Aunt shopping—the two-legged variety."

"Who? Me?" Stacy fanned her lashes with childish innocence. "I asked her to dinner, not to your wedding."

"Don't play innocent. I've told you—"

"You told me you were lonely."

Ben opened his mouth to refute the statement.

"Don't deny it. The other night when I couldn't sleep, and asked you to sit with me you said you understood 'cause sometimes you got lonely, too."

"Stacy, I was reassuring you," Ben replied, his patience stretching near its limit. He glanced in the rear-view mirror to make certain Joyce turned the corner. Her sporty red Mustang convertible followed closely.

He halfway expected her to roar past him at any moment. She wasn't the type of woman to follow any man's lead. She'd certainly cut Bubba down to size without so much as raising her voice.

Unable to resist, he checked his mirror for a second time. Joyce yanked off her baseball cap to free her hair. She appeared to laugh when the wind caught strands of it, whipping it around her face. Sunshine on white silk, Ben mused appreciatively. The lady was the most feminine, sensuous . . . *contrary* woman he'd met in ages.

She isn't your type, he reminded himself. Too assertive. Remembering how flustered she'd been the other evening, he grinned, correcting himself. Independent suited her better. She was the kind of woman who could step into a man's shoes and never break stride. Woe to anyone who stepped on her toes.

She was smart. Tough to *out*-smart. There's a difference, he analyzed, fully aware that he'd tried to best her by volunteering for the distasteful chores required for the baseball team. She hadn't blinked an eye, or blushed, or shrugged, or shredded the paper. As Stacy would say, "She'd kept her cool."

MacIntyre. Wasn't that Irish? So much for the theory that Irish women had a temper. Being of Italian descent on his mother's side, he'd learned to guard against voicing his quick temper. When she'd refused to ride with him, he'd wanted to scream, "Woman, get in. No backtalk!"

And yet, in all fairness, she was also the kind of woman who made a man's heart thud against his rib cage. Her eyes sparkled with humor and a pinch of mischievousness. A sort of "catch me if you can" sparkle. Those long, tanned, shapely legs of hers would be a traffic stopper if she'd wear short shorts. Bermudas didn't do them justice. A T-shirt two sizes smaller wouldn't be a bad idea either. Braless, he added, completing a revised edition to his mental picture.

No, he assured himself without conviction, Joyce wasn't his type. He enjoyed trying to keep a step ahead of her, but that was purely a mental exercise. She was a challenge.

Silently Ben groaned. Mathematicians loved challenges. He'd have to be careful . . . very careful.

"Uncle Ben, are you heartbroken 'cause Petula quit calling at all hours of the night?"

Ben grinned and squeezed Stacy's knee. "No, honey, I'm not heartbroken."

"I didn't think you were. She's kinda pretty, but she had awful telephone manners. Nobody is supposed to make a phone call after nine o'clock."

"Don't criticize your elders, Stacy," he automatically corrected. "She's my secretary. Business calls are perfectly acceptable."

Petula seldom made a decision without consulting her boss. Much as her dependence on him stroked his male ego, there were times when he found her clinging-vine routine slightly annoying. Her midnight calls had driven him nuts.

"She walks funny, too. Kinda like somebody had pinched her buns." Stacy made a sashaying move with her shoulders and hips.

"I hadn't noticed," Ben glibly replied, mentally comparing Petula's mincing steps to Joyce's confident stride. Petula came in a poor second.

"Now who's playing innocent and telling fibs?" Stacy muttered, unbuckling her seatbelt as they pulled into the driveway. She jumped from the car the instant it stopped, yelling, "Mrs. Shane! We've got special company for dinner."

Life is never boring with Stacy around, Ben thought, amused. At times like this he realized how boring his life had been before he'd taken custody of her. Now, he wasn't certain who was in custody of whom.

As he opened his door, Joyce pulled in behind his Cherokee.

She reached under her front seat for her purse and pulled out a wide-toothed comb. "Just a second," she called to Ben.

She felt like a grubby street urchin. With her windblown hair, and barely a trace of lipstick on her mouth, she looked closer to Stacy's age than Ben's. All she needed were Band-Aids on her knees to qualify as Stacy's oversized twin.

Joyce made a face at her reflection in the mirror over the visor. She'd heard others describe her as the healthy, wholesome, girl-next-door type. Hard as she tried, her efforts to appear chic and sophisticated were doomed. Just once she'd like to have someone other than an eight-year-old call her a sexy blond bombshell.

Watching Joyce comb her hair, Ben could feel his temperature rising. Offhand he could think of a hundred or so lovely things he could do with her hair. Hiking it up to the crown of her head

71

and putting a rubber band around it wasn't one of them.

"Leave it down," he requested softly. He caught a glimmer of her combative gaze and added, "Please."

She'd disobey an order from him in a flash. But the magical word, please, changed everything. Her hands dropped limply to the steering wheel. Her hair cascaded over her shoulders, parting naturally in the middle.

"C'mon, Uncle Ben!" Stacy called from the front porch. "Dinner's on the table."

Ben's hand lightly touched the small of Joyce's back, guiding her toward the sidewalk. Her hand accidentally brushed against his thigh. Circuit completed, electricity tingled from the back of her hand to her spine. What to do with her hands was becoming a major problem. Of their own accord, they made contact with Ben at the slightest opportunity.

Stacy saved her by jumping down the steps and grabbing her hand. "Mrs. Shane takes care of me when Uncle Ben isn't here. You'll like her. She isn't bossy, or crabby, or anything."

Ben reluctantly moved his hand to the doorknob. Camouflaged under her baggy T-shirt, he felt certain there was a slender waist. One he could span with his hands.

"What Stacy means is she's the boss when I'm gone," Ben clarified.

"I don't boss Mrs. Shane around," Stacy protested with a giggle.

Ben leaned close to Joyce's ear and whispered, "Her giggle is a dead give away. She can't fib without giggling."

"It's not nice to whisper," Stacy said, tugging Joyce through the center hallway before she could take more than a quick look at the living room on the left and the formal dining room on her right. "How come grownups have different rules than kids? You guys fib and say you're using tacks."

"Tact," Ben corrected. "Stacy hasn't mastered the difference between being tactful and being blunt."

Stacy shrugged her small shoulders. "A fib is a fib. Some of them are little white ones and some of them are big black ones—but they're still fibs, Uncle Ben."

Mrs. Shane bustled from the stove to the table with a hot casserole between twin potholders. At one glance Joyce could see why Stacy liked her. Gray hair pulled back in a bun, plump, with a frilly white apron around her waist, and her blue eyes dancing with good humor, she exuded warmth and love. She was every child's image of a kindly grandmother.

"Mrs. Shane, I'd like you to meet the manager of the Astros, Ms. Joyce MacIntyre."

Stacy glanced from Mrs. Shane to her uncle for

approval of her formal introduction. Mrs. Shane patted her shoulders. Ben grinned with pride.

"Nice meeting you, Ms. MacIntyre," Mrs. Shane greeted. "You're Stacy's favorite topic of conversation."

"She speaks highly of you, too," Joyce answered, feeling as though she'd become a charter member in a mutual admiration society.

"I'd like to visit, but I've got to get home." Mrs. Shane glanced from Joyce to the dinette table, to the kitchen stove, to her purse on the built-in desk. She stripped the apron from her waist and hung it on the pantry door. "Homemade chocolate ice cream for dessert. Everything else is on the table. Sit down and eat."

Stacy wrapped her arms around Mrs. Shane's hips. "See you tomorrow."

Stooping, Mrs. Shane returned the hug and whispered, "You're a sweetheart."

Watching the exchange, Joyce felt a lump rise in her throat.

With the wink of an eye, Mrs. Shane departed, reminding Stacy not to gulp her food down.

"Do you mind if I wash my hands at the kitchen sink?" Joyce asked, turning her hands palms up. "How about your hands, Stacy?"

"Mine are almost clean." She wiped them on her shorts, then held them up for inspection.

"Uh-huh. Let's get the 'almost' off," Ben chuckled, then bribed, "You can be in charge of the liquid soap."

74

"All right!" Stacy pulled a stool to the sink and turned the faucet on. "Hold 'em out, Joyce. You, too, Uncle Ben." Reading the label on the plastic bottle, as she squeezed blobs in their palms, she said, "Here's some Joy for you, and you, and me."

Playfully Stacy and Ben fought for space under the stream of water. Joyce joined in the game. Soon they were washing each other's hands as well as their own. Droplets of water splattered on the countertop as Stacy shook her fingertips and stepped off the stool.

Somehow, Joyce wasn't quite certain how, her hands were between Ben's.

Sensuously he lathered one hand, then the other, paying particular attention to the insides of each finger.

"I haven't had someone wash my hands for me in years," Joyce said. Wet and wild thoughts made her voice whispery. Low in the pit of her stomach she felt hunger pangs that had nothing to do with the aroma coming from the casserole on the table.

Ben grinned, saying boldly, "Showers are better."

A mental image of Ben's lathered hands slithering over her shoulders, breasts, and waist intensified the achy pangs centered between her thighs. Joyce squeezed her legs together to quiet them.

"Come on, slowpokes. I'm starving," Stacy

protested, scraping her chair back from the table. "How long does it take to wash your hands?"

As though he'd forgotten Stacy was in the room, Ben straightened and glanced over his shoulder. "Squeaky clean," he pronounced to Joyce in a totally different tone.

Joyce couldn't muster her thoughts. She barely held on to the paper towel Ben placed in her hands.

Besotted. An old-fashioned expression that aptly fit the dreamy way she reacted to him. *Completely besotted* she added, wiping her hands.

Over dinner Joyce discovered Ben worked at NASA in the research development center. He listened intently about her involvement in the community center's gymnastic program. Although Ben worked out occasionally on the Nautilus equipment, their paths hadn't crossed. They both led active lives that ran in circles that hadn't touched until the present baseball season.

"May I be excused, please?" Stacy asked, finishing her dinner in record time.

"Don't you want dessert?" Ben asked.

"Later. I think Pris is waiting for me in the clubhouse. Can I please be excused?" she pleaded.

Ben nodded. "Wait a minute, young lady. Do you have homework?"

"Uh-uh." Stacy jumped from her chair and hopped from foot to foot.

"Okay. Scat. Don't . . ." The back door

banged loudly. ". . . slam the screen door," he completed, a wry smile on his face.

Joyce forked a bite of the casserole. Her hand stopped midway between the plate and her mouth when she saw Ben's eyes focused on her lips. Her lips parted. She slid the bite into her mouth. Up and down, she coached her jaws. Her automatic reflexes failed. The food melted; she swallowed.

"Good?" Ben asked.

Brown sugar coated her taste buds. Sweet, but not nearly as sweet as the winsome smile curving his lips. Her toes curled inside her canvas sneakers. She was reacting like a rank amateur, but she was worldly enough to know that Ben Williams wanted to kiss her. And she wanted his kiss—desperately.

"The best," she murmured, playing cat and mouse with a slice of wiener and several beans.

Her eyes settled on his lips, waiting for them to move. Her legs crossed and uncrossed. His head tilted a teeny bit; hers synchronized, tilting in the opposite direction.

"Stacy's favorite."

The softer tone of his melodious voice encouraged her to lean forward, to listen carefully, to watch for signs that he wanted to stop making social chitchat and move toward an intimate conversation.

Her lips pursed and hummed, "Hm-hm,"

77

when she wanted to get right down to the fundamentals of their game: kissing.

His knee touched hers; her hand covered his. The dark centers of his eyes widened, pulling her closer.

"You have sauce right . . ." His index finger touched the corner of her mouth. ". . . here."

Certain there wasn't, she exclaimed, "Oh?"

Her parted lips, the excuse he'd fabricated and she'd accepted, were enough. His long fingers curled on her nape beneath her long swath of moonlight-colored hair.

"I'll get it."

His warm, moist breath misted over her lips. Hers trembled as an exquisite arrow of pleasure shot from her lips, to her hand covering his knee, and reverberated at the center of her femininity. His mouth covered hers. The tip of his tongue traced an erotic path to and from the corners of her lips.

The velvet touch of his tongue parted her lips, sampling the brown sugar sweetness of her mouth. It foraged restlessly, hungrily, aimlessly, until her tongue swirled around his, acknowledging his right to be there.

He wasn't stealing a base—she'd purposely walked him to first base—maybe second?

His thumb massaged the back of her neck until she felt pliant, then swept her hair back from her face, twining long strands between his fingers. Sunshine and silk came into his mind again. He could smell it, feel it, relish it. A moan of pleasure rumbled from his chest.

His arm crossed her shoulder, drawing her closer until the tips of her breasts scarcely touched him. Her eyes closed tighter as her nipples hardened, beckoning a closer embrace. Rhythmically he thrust his tongue back and forth, back and forth, until tiny sounds came from her throat.

His lips, moist from hers, moved across her flushed cheek to the sensitive spot beneath her ear. "I want to taste more of you. Here." His tongue laved her small pinkish lobe. His breath spun in the shell of her ear. "Here."

"Yes," Joyce sighed, arching her neck, arching her full breasts against the hard wall of his chest. Her hand came from beneath the table and circled the width of his shoulder. She sat on the corner of her chair, clinging to him as though in danger of falling.

His hand moved until the heel of it touched the underside of her breast. "And here. I want to taste your nipples, feel them bud between my lips. See them." His palm cupped, thumb skating over the diamond-hard tip, circling it, pressing against it. "Oh, woman, it's hard, lush, covered with lace."

His lips suckled her lobe as though they were drawing her nipple into the hot dampness of his mouth. Joyce dug her nails into the hollow of his spine. Her head spun dizzily from his enticing words and the desire to fulfill his wish. She ached. Her knees clung together unable to quell the moist achiness.

"I don't wanna play dolls at your house," they both heard Stacy's voice carrying from the patio. "I wanna play my new baseball video game. C'mon, Pris. We played silly ol' dolls yesterday."

Joyce freed his shoulders and twisted back on her chair. She clasped her hands tightly on her lap to help her sustain the shock of being separated from Ben. When she faced him, she saw he was having an equal amount of difficulty resuming a normal pose for his niece to see when she entered through the back door. His hand dove through his hair, then slid down his chest, settling on his bare thigh.

"Pris, you're being stubborn." She spun around as she closed the door and asked, "Uncle Ben, don't you think it's only fair to give in once in a while and do what the other person wants to do?"

His dark eyes held amusement as they bounced from Stacy to Joyce. "I think that's fair," he replied. "Joyce, do you want some more?"

Joyce wanted more. She craved more kisses, more caresses, more softspoken intimate words.

Unaware of the silent meaning of what Ben was saying to Joyce, Stacy looked at the plate full of food in front of Joyce. "She hasn't eaten what you gave her. Beans and wienies are good, but they fill you up real fast. I'm always hungry for more half an hour after I've eaten." She put one hand on her hip and shook her finger toward Joyce. "Don't let him bully you into taking a bigger helping than you can eat. He'll make you sit there until your plate is empty."

Ben and Joyce chuckled. Sparkles of delight passed between them.

Priscilla edged toward the table. "Mr. Williams, my mom wants to know if Stacy can go out for pizza tomorrow and sleep over tomorrow night?"

"Please, Uncle Ben," Stacy begged.

Ben considered the request for half a second, smiling lazily at Joyce. "Sounds like fun."

Both girls jumped up and down, squealing, dashing toward Stacy's bedroom to play the video games.

"Stacy has ball practice Saturday morning at ten," Ben called after them. "I'll come and get her."

When the girls were out of earshot, he quoted Stacy teasing, "Are beans and wienies more filling than kisses?"

Joyce toyed with the food on her plate. "How would I know? I haven't had my fill of . . ." she paused and winked, ". . . either."

"Are you going to be hungry half an hour after you've eaten?"

Flames hidden deep within his dark eyes told her that he was still hungry to taste her, to hell with what was on his plate.

"I'm not certain I'll be satisfied without a second helping," she quipped, enjoying the innuendos lurking behind what could pass as idle dinner conversation.

"I wouldn't want to bully you."

Joyce grinned. "I wouldn't let you."

CHAPTER FIVE

Ben tossed his napkin on the table after they'd finished their dinner. "Stacy does the dishes."

"Woman's work?" Joyce asked, chuckling.

"Nope. A routine lesson in responsibility. It's my turn next week." His expression sobered. "I take my responsibility for Stacy seriously. I'd like nothing more than to coax you into the family room and continue where we were before we were so rudely interrupted. Frankly, necking on the sofa while Stacy is still awake leaves a lot to be desired. You've made one helluva impact on me, but . . ."

Joyce heard his voice trail off into nothingness. Was he giving her the brush-off?

"But," he continued, his eyes sparkling with anticipation, "there's tomorrow night. My social etiquette is a bit rusty. Is it too late to ask you for a date?"

Joyce liked the idea of his being socially rusty. That meant he wasn't involved with another woman. She disliked the idea of a formal date.

Selfishly she didn't want to share him with a crowd in a movie theater, or a restaurant, or any other public place. She wanted to be alone with him. Very, very alone.

"My social calendar has a vacant spot or two. Tomorrow would be wonderful. Why don't we grill a couple of steaks and relax around the pool in my backyard?"

Ben lifted her hand and raised it to his lips. "I can't think of anything I'd enjoy more."

"You remember how to get there?"

"I'll find your house." *And you,* his eyes said. "What time?"

"Sixish?"

"I'll be there," he promised. She followed his train of thought as he glanced toward the plaid sofa in the adjoining room. "I'm having second thoughts about you and me going into the family room."

"No doors," she protested mentally gauging the repercussions of Stacy finding her uncle and the manager of her baseball team stretched out on the sofa. "I don't think Stacy would understand."

Ben chuckled. "Oh, she'd understand, all right. I'm certain you're aware of how progressive Texas schools are."

"Not that progressive," Joyce disclaimed, "at least not in the second or third grade." Their conversation drifting toward the topic of school reminded Joyce of a stack of ungraded test papers on her desk at home. She hated the thought of leaving, but realized it was the smart thing to do. Sexual tension was strung so tightly between them she could hear it humming in her ears. She rose, sliding the chair back with her knees. "I've got to go."

"Wait," he ordered. Misunderstandings were too easily turned into barriers. He wanted no barriers between them. "I didn't mean that as a slam against the local school district."

Joyce grinned. "I didn't take what you said in an unfavorable light. I have papers to grade and lesson plans to prepare. During the last couple of weeks of school those 'progressive teachers' you mentioned are counting on me to help them hold the roof on the school building by exhausting the kids during PE."

"They do get hyperactive, don't they? Stacy is like an overwound spring." Rising, he looped his arm across her shoulders, "I'll walk you to your car."

Hips and thighs brushed, igniting small explosions of awareness.

She wasn't surprised when Ben paused at the door. Outside, standing in the driveway with the late-evening sun making every look, every gesture openly observable, wasn't where they should part. They'd come too far for a jaunty wave of the hand to satisfy either of them.

His guiding hand turned her around at the door, resting lightly on her slender waist. Wistfully he said, "It's early for a good-night kiss, isn't it?"

"Our table talk was . . . unusual. I'd say a precedent has been set." Oddly, as her fingers spread and climbed up his chest, she felt as though she were home instead of going home. "Kiss me?"

"Is that an order?" He closed the gap between them. He ducked his head, nuzzled her neck, locating the soft vulnerable below her ear with unerring accuracy.

She ignored his question. Pinned between the hard wall and his chest, she melted. He nipped the throbbing pulse on her throat with a sharp love bite.

Physical education teachers were required to take extensive college course work in biological sciences. Her limited experience with men added to her knowledge of the male anatomy. But nothing prepared her for the ready evidence of his manliness. His rigidity pressed against her unabashedly.

"Should I be embarrassed?" he asked when he felt her shudder against him. "I can't remember when a woman has made me lose control."

Glad she was the woman who'd had that effect on him, she groaned, her hips arching involuntarily forward. His strong hands lowered to her hips, sustaining her movement. Slowly kneading her derriere with maddening results. "You're having a powerful effect on me, too," she confessed. "My insides are tingling."

"You're so damned cute and sexy, especially when you're trying to show me who's boss."

Cute, yes. Sexy? Miss-Wholesome-America, sexy? Even if he was fibbing she wanted to hear every single word.

"I hate the thought of your leaving. If it were possible, I'd carry you into my bedroom and find the source of that tingling sensation."

He lifted his head and she became lost in his near-black eyes. She realized, without a doubt, that she'd go willingly.

"Pay close attention," he mouthed against her lips. "This is what you do to me."

Suddenly conscious of how fleeting this moment could be, he wasted no time. His mouth hotly claimed hers. His tongue dove masterfully between her lips. He buried himself inside of her in a sensuous imitation of how their loving would be if only . . .

If only we were alone, Joyce thought, parrying each thrust of his tongue. Belly rubbed belly. Man against woman. Hardness mating with pliant softness.

Her senses reeled with the imagery painted across the backs of her lids. One of them had to stop, to be sensible. He'd admitted he'd lost control. She had to tamp down her desire. The heels of her hands moved between them. Pushing,

87

once, twice, she heard him groan, knew what stopping was costing him.

He braced his hands against the wall and shoved himself backward. "Woman, I hope this isn't just fun and games for you."

Revealing his anxiety, his doubts, his vulnerability gave Joyce unlimited power over him. She gave it back.

"No games," she promised. Blindly reaching behind herself, she found the doorknob, twisted it, and opened the door. "No games."

She slipped through the opening and was gone in a flash.

Her hair whipped wildly around her shoulders as she drove toward the Gulf Freeway. Humming along with the radio, she didn't have a care in the world. She relived each intimate touch, yearning for more. Tossing her head back, she laughed with glee.

Four o'clock the next day, she grimaced, pacing between balance beams. Spellbound by Ben, she'd completely forgotten the special practice she'd made to several promising students. Ten-year-olds were bounding from the gymnasium floor to the strategically placed balance beams. Hot and sweaty, she glanced at the clock on the wall.

Another hour of practice, a twenty-minute drive, and a quick stop at the grocery store to pick up steaks would barely leave her time to spray cologne on her wrists. She'd tried unsuccessfully to call Ben. He must be the only person in the world who didn't have a recording device on his telephone.

Having spent the night tossing and turning, she felt as rumpled as her unmade bed at home. Mentally, she compared Ben's home with hers. Mrs. Shane kept Ben's home, literally, dust-proof. Everything had a place and that's where it was.

Her home was fairly clean, but cluttered. Generous assessment, Joyce chided. Pantyhose hanging from the bar in the shower, clothes tossed everywhere, a pile of soiled linen in front of the washer—very generous, indeed.

In the extra hour and a half she'd spent at school, she could have zipped around and had everything spotless. She realized, too late, she should have stayed up until the wee hours of the morning until her house had sparkled, but she hadn't. She'd been too busy grading papers, *giggling,* planning relay games, *hugging herself,* and being downright *foolish!* Today she was paying the price.

The messiness inside her home compared unfavorably with Mrs. Shane's housekeeping. However, the insides of her body exactly matched her cluttered home. A whole covey of quail had taken up residence in her stomach. Each time she thought of Ben, they flapped their wings. Each time she blew the whistle, hanging from a strip of leather around her neck, it sounded like Bob White, Bob White. At any moment she expected the quail to take flight, with disgraceful results. Her nervous stomach was extremely queasy.

"Roberta, arch your back," she called to a small girl stiffly spreading her arms and raising one leg. "Watch it. Don't rush or you'll lose your balance."

Good advice, teach, she inwardly mocked, knowing she'd violated that essential fundamental principle for fledgling gymnasts. In the love game, she certainly qualified as fledgling material. She'd crammed teaching, coaching, and tutoring into her schedule since graduating from college. There had been sporadic occasions when she'd dated, but nothing serious.

Ben Williams and serious dating were one and the same.

He'd made the rules: no game playing, no hitting below the belt.

She'd observe his rules, but she wanted his rules clarified. No game playing took their relationship beyond the one-night-stand level, didn't it? Leading someone on was hitting below the belt, for certain.

Joyce guarded her heart, not freely giving it to any man. But, Ben wasn't "any man"; he was special. With her feet flat on the ground, he could make her feel as if she'd completed a full somersault, landed on the beam and gracefully executed a split. Nearly an impossible feat, especially for a woman who admitted to being inexperienced.

Unable to endure her silent qualms or the snail's-pace movement of the clock's hands, she dismissed class fifteen minutes early. If nothing else, she'd have time to pick up around the house and give her furniture a lick and a promise. Maybe she'd squeeze in a quick dip in the pool. Despite her distressed state, she wanted to give the appearance of being calm, cool, and sophisticated.

For the next forty-five minutes, she did a perfect imitation of a film projector set on fast forward. Alice in Wonderland's White Rabbit hopping along lickety-split would have been panting and gasping to keep up with her. Inside her head, Joyce silently sang, "I'm late. I'm late, for a very important date. No time to say 'hello' 'good-bye', I'm late, I'm late, I'm late!"

Her fingers shook as she struggled with the back clasp of the ruffled top of her white bikini. Each of the three rows of gathered ruffles was piped in varying shades of hot pink. Stepping barefooted into the scant bottoms, with enticing bows that matched the colorful piping on the top, she wondered if the swimsuit was too daring, too risqué. Until now, she'd worn it only in the secluded privacy of her own pool, without guests.

Finger parting her hair in the back, she pulled it over her breasts to minimize her bareness. One peek in the mirror and she flounced it over her shoulders. Her waist-length hair brought forward, veiling her top in shimmering whiteness,

91

gave her the appearance of being naked from the waist up.

The front doorbell pealed.

Too late to chicken out. She grabbed a lacy coverup from the dresser drawer, hastily tugged it on, and scampered toward the door.

"Coming," she shouted, giving each room a quick once-over with her eyes. Everything appeared neat and tidy. God help him if he opened a cabinet or pulled out a drawer!

Taking a deep breath, she swung the front door open wide.

"Hi," Ben said, strangling the casual greeting through his paralyzed vocal cords. Gone were the baggy shorts and T-shirt, replaced by a delectable sugar cobweb of lace confection. His mathematical heart tripped double time as he mentally tabulated her measurements.

"Come in."

Her invitation stirred him like a gust of hot desert air on naked skin. He hadn't embarrassed her yesterday, but for damned sure his masculine reaction today would make her believe his aroused state was perpetual.

Joyce openly stared at him. His white terry-cloth shirt hung open, exposing a wealth of dark chest hair. The black collar matched his swim trunks. His feet were bare. Simple, but devastating, she mused. In his hand he held a bottle of wine. Tiny droplets trickled from the bottle and splashed on her polished toenails.

"Brrrr. Cold," she commented, taking the chilled bottle.

A winsome grin tugged at the corners of Ben's mouth. "Cold? I'm in danger of burning up right before your very eyes. You're gorgeous."

Boldly, Joyce rose on tiptoe and kissed his clean-shaven jaw. "Thanks for not giggling." His baffled expression made her explain. "Remember? You said Stacy always giggles when she tells a fib."

He chuckled, letting her lead the way. He could follow her to the gates of hell without noticing anything other than the sexy sway of her hair over her rounded bottom. Her long shapely legs weren't anything to giggle over either.

"Want to swim before or after?" she asked she blurted, aware of his eye closely following her. Her hands fluttered aimlessly. The bottle began to slip in her hand. Inwardly groaning at her breathlessness and the unintentional innuendo, she added, "Before or after we eat."

"A cool dip might restore my appetite for food," he responded honestly, then weakly joked, "Maybe not. I have this vague notion that once you remove your coverup, I may need mouth-to-mouth resuscitation."

"I'll put the wine in an ice bucket and bring it poolside. You go ahead to the pool." One hand flittered from her chest, toward the pool, and returned to her chest. Amusement lit his dark eyes.

She smiled. "I've been flighty as a quail during bird season."

"Sweetheart, from the amount of Alka-Seltzer I've consumed today, my head should be fizzing," he confessed, leveling his eyes on hers. "We're both exhausting ourselves worrying what the other one will think. Why don't you get the bucket and wineglasses? I'll get the ice. That'll keep both our hands temporarily too busy to get into trouble."

Grinning, Joyce swept her coverup aside and placed one hand on her hip. "Was that an order, Coach?"

"A suggestion. It hasn't been ten seconds since you told me to go jump in the pool." His eyebrows lifted, following the enticing curve of her waist and hips. "But my libido has some explicit orders, if you'd care to listen."

Genuinely laughing, she shook her head. "No orders from you or your devilish libido. Get the ice . . . *please.*"

Ben pulled the freezer drawer open. "Tell me, what's an attractive single woman doing living away from town, alone?"

"I've always lived here." She sank to her haunches and rummaged in the back of a cabinet for an ice bucket. "My parents retired several years ago and bought two condos. One in Corpus, where they winter and one on Cape Cod, where they spend the summer. They didn't have the heart to sell this house."

"Were your parents educators?"

Joyce chuckled. His familiarity with the retirement program for Texas teachers must be nil, she mused, knowing she couldn't afford two places on her present income. "No. Ever hear of MacIntyre Paper Company?"

"Sorry, can't say that I have."

Silently she blessed NASA for being the proverbial ivory tower in Texas. She wasn't sensitive regarding her parents' wealth, but she recalled Stacy saying Ben wouldn't allow her to discuss M-O-N-E-Y. Although her house was unpretentious, the athletic facilities in the backyard were worth more than several gold watches buried under the front porch.

Locating the bucket, she gracefully arose. "Dad's a stereotype 'good ol' boy' who worked diligently for forty years." She centered the wine in the bucket and gestured for him to dump the ice around it. "I have glasses in the bar outside."

Joyce led him through the dinette area to the rear door.

"You didn't tell me your father was the only Japanese MacIntyre in America," he said, awestruck by the five-lane pool with a wooden bridge arching into a circular diving tank. A spacious cabana nestled in a grouping of tall pines. The entire area was alive with native wildflowers placed in flowerbeds lined with sandstone. Inviting aqua-blue chaise longues lined the pool. Privacy was insured by the eight-foot-high wooden fence. "Aren't they famous for having simple homes with fabulous backyards?"

Laughing, Joyce set the ice bucket on the patio table. "Yeah, but Dad and Mom are pure Irish, raised with a Texan's love for rugged independence. If anything, he's a reincarnated fish. He loves water."

"Who's the diver?"

"Mostly my older brother, Sean, who's taken over Dad's business." No longer self-conscious, she shed her coverup. "Sean's a character."

Ben concentrated on keeping his eyes above her neck. "How so?"

"He's investigating the practicality of paper clothes," she replied, edging close to the edge of the pool. Aware of what would happen to her bikini top if she dove in, she slowly went down the steps. "I think he got the idea from one of his ex-girlfriends who writes bodice rippers."

"Disposable clothing," Ben mused aloud, intrigued by the practicality of paper swimsuits. Paper melted into nothingness when dampened. He pushed the dangerous thought aside.

Content to languish in the shoulder-deep water, Joyce leaned her head back against the natural stone coping and said, "Swim a few laps if you want. I'm going to be lazy."

Ben watched her eyes close. Relaxed, she floated to the surface. One look and he dove into the water. Swim, swim, swim, you horny toad, he coached mercilessly.

Through slitted lashes, droplets of water caught the rainbow's colors as she watched Ben slice through the water. Normally, she'd have noticed whether or not his strokes were in good form. She didn't care about his strokes. From the furtive glances she taken, she knew he was physically in top form.

His head ducked beneath the surface, then bobbed up. "Is there a tunnel between the two pools?"

Too lackadaisical to exert energy, she merely nodded.

Ben swam through the tunnel into the diving tank, then back again. Holding his breath until his lungs burned, he swam underwater until he was beside Joyce. With one arm positioned beneath her knees, the other bracing her shoulders, he surfaced, holding her.

Gasping in surprise, she grabbed hold of his neck. "No ducking allowed."

"I wouldn't duck you," Ben teased, releasing her legs. He stood flat-footed, but he knew she couldn't touch bottom. She drifted against him.

Her nose tickled as it rubbed against the wet hairs on his chest. "You're disturbing my rest," she faintly protested.

His skin was sleek. Her hands familiarized themselves with the hollow of his spine, and the hollow of his collarbone. The fragrance of his tangy cologne mingled pleasantly with a hint of chlorine. *Irresistible,* she thought, licking a drop that clung to his jaw.

Amused, but feeling the stirring in his loins, he dropped a chaste kiss on her lips, then walked her to the pool's edge. "I'll pour the wine."

In one fluid motion, he surged from the pool.

Eyes closed, she heard him lift the lid on the gas grill. Seconds later, a cork popped. Light music from the stereo system played. Joyce smiled at the pleasant thought of Ben making himself at home. Only the sound of glasses chiming against each other alerted her to his approach.

"Some layout," Ben said, admiring the hint of cleavage his height awarded him.

His hands itched to discover the feel of liquid ivory silk. He eased into the pool. Pouring the effervescent wine, he couldn't resist temptation. He dribbled golden drops of the chilled wine into the enticing shadow between her breasts. "I'm returning the favor," he said huskily as his lips and the tip of his tongue followed the leisurely course of the wine. Tilting his head until she could see one of his eyes, he murmured, "Hmm. Good vintage year."

An ache grew inside of her, coiling tighter and tighter with each touch of his velvet tongue. She wanted him closer, much closer. Of their own accord, her legs wrapped around his waist.

"There isn't much to this suit, but what there is I wish were made of dissolvable paper."

"Is that a hint, Mr. Williams?"

98

His dark head raised, eyes flashing a devilish brilliance. "I did happen to notice that you're missing something."

"What?"

"Suntan lines. Just per chance, does the prim and proper manager of the Astros sunbathe in the nude?"

Joyce slowly smiled. "It's very secluded here."

"Hmm." Ben fiddled with the clasp to her top. Frustrated, he asked, "How the hell do you work the clasp?"

"You're the mathematician," she provocatively replied. "You figure it out."

"The designer used a formula I'm unfamiliar with," he whispered, teasing the ruffled edge with his tongue, nudging it lower and lower. A low groan passed through his lips as one rosy nipple, tight as a bud, seemed to wink at him. The clasp magically separated. His fingers discarded her top, setting it adrift. "No tan marks . . . any-where?"

"Uh-huh."

In seconds, he'd untied the tiny bows at the sides of her suit and cast them aside. She watched the dark centers of his eyes expand as he gazed through the sparkling, transparent water. "You're sexy as hell. You know that, don't you?" The heel of his hand covered her blond curls. His fingers swishing over her abdomen drove coher-ent thought from her mind. His hips gently rocked in the cradle of her thighs, making silky waves lap between them.

"Now I do," she murmured.

"What are you thinking, sweetheart?" he asked when a smile flickered across her lips.

"I'm wondering if you have tan marks." She twined her arms around his neck, loosening her legs, letting them slide down his length.

"I do," he wryly admitted. "Stacy . . ."

His hands stroked, his lips teased, but he didn't take the hint. She lightly snapped the elasticized band at his waist.

"Aren't you . . . ?"

"No."

"Why? Fair is fair, Coach."

His forehead rocked against hers. "Because . . ."

"Now who's being prim and proper?" she chided, brushing her breasts against his chest. "Making love only takes place at night? Between sweet-smelling sheets?"

"Yeah," he admitted with a cheeky grin. "My fantasies are a bit conservative."

"Reality can be better," she promised, echoing the movement of her shoulders. Her lips teased, tantalized, but refused anything more than the barest of kisses. "Creativity and spontaneity have a lot going for them."

She felt his hands leave her waist. His hips shimmied. His dark trunks floated away. His eyes lost their teasing light. His hands settled low on her hips, pulling her forward as he turned his back against the side of the pool. Thick and hard, he let her drift lazily against him.

"New rules," he whispered softly. "Yours."

"Uh-uh. We'll have to make them up as we go along."

"Does that mean what I think it means?"

"Probably. I've never made love in the pool, either," she confessed, sighing.

Ben tossed his head back and laughed with delight. "We're going to drown. You know that, don't you?"

"Gonna be a quitter?" she teased.

He swallow her taunt with a hot, stifling kiss. This would be a first—for both of them.

CHAPTER SIX

Joyce rolled over on her stomach and pulled her pillow over her head, ignoring the hand gently shaking her shoulder.

"Sweetheart?"

Her mother called her sweetheart. *Mama, how your voice has changed,* she mused with a satiated smile. She hadn't slept this well in years. "In a minute," she answered groggily.

Ben lifted a tangled lock of her hair and painted lazy eights on her back. "You're going to be late for ball practice."

Groaning, Joyce blinked owlishly. Her mother might pull her big toe to get her out of bed, but she'd never brushed her hair down her spine in such an exotic pattern. Her toes curled under with delight as her hand moved to the left. Her mother wouldn't be in her bed, nor did she have hair on her chest.

Sighing, vividly remembering in glorious detail how she'd spent the night, Joyce peeked from under the pillow. "Morning, Ben."

"Slow starter?" Ben asked, removing the pillow, loving how her hand draped over his shoulder to draw him closer.

"No coffee . . . no Wheaties—the breakfast of champions," she grumped between yawns. She stretched, rolled to her back and grinned up at Ben. "No alarm clock bell ringing to get me away from the starting line."

"Isn't this better?" He circled the pinkish-brown tips of her breasts, dabbing his version of an artist's brush here and there.

"Mmm, infinitely. But it doesn't make me want to spend the day coaching baseball."

Her nipples budded under his pleasant ministrations. He circled her waist. "We're supposed to be there in a couple of hours."

"Plenty of time," she said, sucking in her stomach by taking a deep breath. His hand spanned the concave width. His eyelids drooped as her palm made similar forays from his chest to his navel. "Feel good?" she asked rhetorically.

"You're one helluva woman, Joyce. Care to cancel practice for today? I'll call Stacy and have her stay at Priscilla's house until Mrs. Shane arrives."

"You're tempting me to neglect my responsibilities," she complained without conviction. "At least you didn't order me to stay in bed."

Ben lowered his head to her breast, moistly kissing the erect tip. "You'd rebel. I'm concentrating on a gentle form of persuasion."

103

"We have to be there. Bubba . . ." Her breath caught as his lips nipped, then pulled her deep into his hot mouth. ". . . won't be there on time. We have to get up."

His thigh curved over hers. Raising his head, he smiled but refused to state the obvious.

"Couple of hours?" she asked, receiving his message, shifting under him, she teased, "We have time for a morning swim. That's a wake-me-up."

"Like hell, woman. I seem to remember your collapsing in my arms after our swim yesterday."

Joyce grinned, remembering the rapture she'd seen on his face. "Yeah, and you loved it."

"We could have drowned," he said, but the smug curve of his mouth charmed her.

He nudged her legs apart, bent her knees on either side of his waist. His hands molded her breasts together, kneading their ripe fullness. Her fingers curled into his hair and pulled him down to her.

"I'm drowning now," she whispered, arching her hips upward with wanton abandonment. The knot of passion low inside her wanted him fast, hard, to take her to the pinnacle of lovemaking. "Take me . . ."

Her head spun dizzily as Ben deftly rolled on his back and took her astride him. Knees bent, toes tucked under his thighs, hands braced on his chest, her hair gloriously covering his shoulders, he said, "That sounded remarkably like a command, sweetheart. Let's reverse it. You take me."

She heard the challenge in his voice. From the previous evening's pillow talk, he knew of her inexperience. Feeling unbalanced, awkward, and yet also feeling liberated from his weight, she whispered, "Open your eyes. Let me watch you with the same intensity you watched me."

His dark eyes garnered the rays of the dim sunlight coming through the windows until the sun's brightness centered in his eyes. She'd follow his order, but at an excruciatingly slow pace. Beneath her, he felt more of a man than when he'd been in the dominate position. His hands locked on her hips, urging her to end the exquisite torment.

Joyce stretched over him. When they'd made love in the pool they'd both been out of their elements. He'd joked about drowning, but his physical strength and agility combined with his uninhibited love talk made their lovemaking as exquisite as it was unique. Now, she was the master.

Between their chests, her silky hair gave a new tactility to flesh on flesh. Like a kitten, she rubbed against him. Her hips swayed in a tantalizing rhythm. Her eyes locked with his. She praised him, hoping she could be as articulate as he had been.

"Your skin feels hot . . . supple against my breasts . . ." Her voice sounded hoarse to her own ears. Sinking against him, she realized she couldn't match his glibness. She was a physical person, one who expressed her inner feelings with her body. What she found difficult to say aloud, she silently communicated with her lips, teeth, and tongue.

She circled the nubs of his masculine nipples with the tip of her tongue. They hardened to stiff points. Surprised that his response was similar to hers, her lips curved as she took him into her mouth. His harsh groan and the tightening of his fingers on her hips made her mouth bolder. She teased, darting quickly, circling languidly, dancing her tongue over the taut peaks. His chest burned from the tiny licking flames she'd started with each flick of her tongue.

"Turgid . . . tangy," she exclaimed between nips, voicing her thoughts, striving to please him.

"Oh, sweetheart," Ben groaned, clenching his teeth to keep from using his superior strength. He could arch his hips, force her sweet hips down upon him, bury himself inside of her. Never had he wanted her more than he wanted her now. Yes, he acknowledged wanting her in a most carnal way, but he also wanted more. He wanted her strength, her will, her soul.

"You're driving me wild. Come to me," he begged.

She peppered kisses up his throat until she reached his lips. They were open. Small pants of moist breath, made sweet with passion, fanned her assuredness. She kissed him with a wildness that inflamed both of them.

Ben crushed her against his chest, hips, thighs. She probed deeply, swirling, tasting, thrusting in and out, evoking a primitive rhythm that matched his pounding heart beneath her hand. Her body writhed against him.

His eyes squeezed closed in an effort to keep himself in check. He wanted to flip her beneath him, plunge into her tight softness. To control himself, he flung his arms wide. His fingers clenched and unclenched.

He had to prove to himself that he could allow her to dominate him and remain her equal. Love was give and take. He wanted her to love him as much as he wanted her to make love to him.

Gradually, when she could no longer bear the twisted knot of passion, she raised on her knees and sank lower on his hips. Sustaining the torment, she slowly opened herself to him. He stretched her, filling her, letting her take all of him as she rocked back to her heels.

She watched. His skin stretched across his cheekbones, making them more pronounced. A small muscle in his jaw tweaked, rebelling against his temperance. His rib cage heaved beneath her hands. His strength of will made her adore him.

Had his eyes been open, he would have seen her love shining brightly as she pumped against him, riding him hard, fast, until his hands coiled around her, holding her while his love poured into her. Being a natural athlete, her gracefulness, strength, and stamina made it possible for her to reach the pinnacle of lovemaking, an exhilarating high. Waves of pleasure washed over her.

She'd dominated. She'd submitted. She'd loved . . . and been loved.

Cradled against his chest, his hands brushed her hair aside and soothed her by stroking her back, following the natural cleft. His lips touched the crown of her head barely moving, kissing, murmuring disjointed phrases.

Ben made her aware that her physical fitness gave her a lithe gracefulness few women possessed. How she walked, her posture, her gestures were lyrical. Confident. Graceful. Perfect. His habit of closely watching her stemmed from his innate need to observe and tabulate. Her measurements were numbers that gave the first clue to her sensuality, but she was too complex to simplify into a formula.

He admitted being physically attracted to her. What man wouldn't be? But the closer he delved into her complexity, he realized that in addition to her loveliness, she was extremely bright. Her sense of humor and quick wit demolished his stereotype of a female jock. Her mental dexterity amazed him. Few people—male or female, egghead or jock—could organize both children and adults into a cooperative group.

She was like a many-faceted precious gem: the closer he studied her, the more she fascinated him. From watching her coach, he knew she seldom lost sight of her goals, but certain values were dear to her. Fairness, individuality, and personal integrity were sacred. She wouldn't sacrifice a child's self-esteem to win a game. She encouraged each player to do their best. And yet, her sense of compassion enabled her to be understanding when a person fell short of their capabilities. When a fielder fumbled, she reminded the player of a spectacular play they'd made. She built confidence. She made the players want to reach a bit farther, run a bit faster, swing harder.

And that's how she made him feel, too. Stronger, more confident, virile. Eager to try the impossible. She challenged him, both mentally and physically.

While he spoke, she cuddled, feeling closer to understanding herself than she'd ever felt. Her entire life, she'd known she was a physical person, but never had she felt as womanly. Her entire collection of trophies were worthless when compared to what he'd given her.

"Score's even," Joyce coached. "No hits. No runs. Batter up."

The smile on her face was a permanent fixture. Regardless of how the kids fumbled the ball, slid into first, or overthrew the bases, the rosy glow left by their early-morning lovemaking kept a constant grin on her face.

She noticed Ben had a similar sappy smile. Another affliction hampered his coaching. He either had a boulder in his eye or he winked when he felt certain no one else was looking.

Bubba growled, "We're gonna be losers if you let them get away with playing sloppy ball. What we ought to do is grab 'em by the scruff of the neck and . . ."

"Shut up, Bubba," Ben said without rancor. "The game is for fun. We don't have any scouts in the bleachers with a pro contract in their pocket. As Stacy would say, 'Chill out, man.' "

Muttering to himself, Bubba pounded the catcher's mitt with his fist.

Joyce had the distinct feeling Bubba wished he'd volunteered to manage the team. His let's-get-tough-and-win philosophy diametrically opposed her methods. Winning was his ultimate goal. Ridicule and criticism were the means he used to reach it.

She'd squelched his philosophy and his tirades with her games-are-fun approach to teaching baseball skills. Team cooperation and playing to the best of one's ability was her goal. She wanted to win, but not when the price for the game was a child's integrity.

She realized Ben calculated the advantages and disadvantages of each method, then found a happy medium. Yes, the batter must wear safety helmets to protect the children from injury. But no, Ben wouldn't voice an opinion when Bubba instructed a child to step into the pitch and Joyce told them to plant their feet solid. Yes, the batter must slide into home plate or be called out by the umpire if the ball was being thrown home. But no, sliding into every base wasn't necessary. He stayed on the pitcher's mound and concentrated on getting the ball across the plate.

One thing she could count on, Ben wouldn't allow Bubba to make condescending remarks about the manager being a woman. Joyce had mixed emotions regarding Ben's protective instincts. The feminine part of her relished having his broad shoulders and authoritative voice providing a buffer between Bubba and herself. And yet, the independent, self-sufficient part of her resented his stepping in when she was perfectly capable of dealing with Bubba. Each part battled with the other for supremacy.

Sonny stepped into the batter's box. Jacob ran up to Joyce, waiting to run.

"I just love to feel my feet touch those bases," little Jacob said, ready to run when Sonny hit the ball.

Joyce glanced at Jacob. The helmet he wore was oversized, wobbling on his head. His shoes were untied. His little legs churned in place. Optimistic as she was, she seriously doubted Jacob would feel the bags under his feet in a real game. He had the grit, but his eye-hand coordination didn't match it. The closest he'd come to hitting the ball was to nick it. But he tried. He avidly loved baseball and that's what Little League was all about: teaching youngsters to love the game.

Ben pitched the ball; Sonny clobbered it.

"Run, Jacob. Touch each base." She made a note on the batting line up page. "Sonny, you'll bat fourth at the opening game."

"Y'hear that, son. You're clean-up batter," Bubba crowed, patting his son's rear end.

Clean-up batter and clean-up parent, Joyce mused. She looked forward with growing anticipation to seeing Bubba bending and stooping to pick up litter from under the bleachers.

Lucille, Jacob's mother and team mother, distracted Joyce from watching Jacob run the bases.

"Can I talk to the boys before they leave?" Lucille asked timidly, clutching a pile of paper to her chest much like Jacob held his glove.

Joyce nodded. "Hustle up here, Astros. Jacob's mother has some papers for you to take home. Listen carefully."

Her eyes automatically drifted in Ben's direction. She'd had trouble during practice keeping her hands and eyes off him. One finger over his lips, he signaled Stacy to quit whispering to Sonny and pay attention.

First love, Joyce mused fondly. She remembered being the same age, wildly infatuated with the team's star player, Buddy Sawyer. He'd nicknamed her Tag-along, for a good reason. She followed him everywhere. Being "just a girl," she had to be better or she wasn't allowed to play.

112

She learned to catch, field, and hit better than Buddy's friends. Encouraged by her father, she imagined herself as the first woman to break into the professional ranks. Buddy would pitch and she'd be catching. They were inseparable, invincible, the Superman and Wonder Woman of the Texas Little League. In her young, trusting eyes she pictured them as man and wife, throwing balls to each other as they headed toward the World Series.

Their Little League team won the trophy that summer. Buddy hugged her. Of course, everybody hugged everybody. And yet, she knew Buddy had held her a second longer, squeezed her a bit tighter than anyone else. She basked in their glory.

By autumn, Buddy deserted her for a football buddy. Football! she'd bemoaned to her father. Her mother put her foot down when she started stuffing herself to gain weight. Playing catcher was one thing, but doubling her weight to qualify as a linebacker was utterly ridiculous.

Joyce watched Stacy and Sonny trade gloves. Careful, little girl, she wanted to warn. Those aren't wedding rings you're exchanging. Guard your heart. It's fragile. Far more easily destroyed than your favorite baseball glove.

Her eyes climbed from Ben's hand, which draped over Stacy's shoulder, to his attentive eyes. A thickness lodged in her throat. Should she be following her own advice? Naïveté wasn't

113

restricted to the young. What would happen between Ben and herself at the end of the baseball season? He'd told her how much he admired her, but Ben hadn't promised anything. Stacy could twist his words and volunteer him for future commitments, but Joyce couldn't.

She watched Sonny poke Stacy and return her glove.

Ben grinned and winked, unaware of the doubts formulating in her mind.

". . . and Mickey's parents are responsible for drinks tickets at the first game," Lucille concluded, bumping Joyce's arm to get her attention.

Joyce swallowed the lump of apprehension lodging in her throat as she foresaw what would happen at the end of baseball season. Ben would thank her for managing the team and walk away from the field . . . without her.

"Joyce? You look a little pale. It's hotter than Hades out here. Are you okay?" Lucille asked.

Blinking her eyes, Joyce obliterated her mental picture. She bounced back to where she was as though she'd momentarily fallen from a beam, but quickly recovered. Her routine questions regarding the next practice session blurted hollowly toward the kids, "When's the next practice?"

"Tuesday."

"Where?"

"At the batting cages."

"Don't forget to bring your money. What time?"

"Five o'clock."

"Sharp. That's it, 'Stros. See you Tuesday."

Amid the shouts of the dispersing team, Joyce heard Stacy say to her uncle, "You promised!"

"Stacy, I said it was a good idea and I'd think about it."

"But, I counted on you to take us." Stacy's lower lip quivered; her blue eyes were awash with tears. "I told Sonny . . ."

"You catch up with Sonny and tell him I've made other plans."

"But, Uncle Ben . . ." Stacy pleaded. "You're always saying that practice makes perfect. They'll kick me off the team if I can't hit the ball. Sonny is the best batter. Sonny says . . ."

Ben was heartily sick of "Sonny says" prefacing every word his niece uttered. "Stop. Now. It's our team's turn for field maintenance. You're the one who volunteered me to coach. Maybe we can go to the batting cages to practice hitting *after* we get the work finished. Go!"

"Mean ol' sidewinder," Stacy muttered, getting the last word if she couldn't get her way. "Always bossin' me around, makin' me do his work."

Joyce pulled the bats from the cyclone fence and put them in the equipment bag. Before Ben had left her house, he'd told her that he had to work on the field after practice. She'd offered to help.

115

"Little problem there, Coach?" she asked, watching Ben stride toward her.

"Yeah. Stacy thinks I'm running a taxicab service. Do you think Stacy will learn to quit volunteering me for everything?" Ben asked, voicing his complaint.

Reluctant to take sides while relatively uninformed, she mouthed a popular child-rearing platitude: "Be consistent."

"Easier said than done, sweetheart." Ben lifted the bag to his shoulder. "She has her mother's stubborn streak."

"The Williams men aren't stubborn?"

Ben grinned, remembering how his mother swore that the Williams men had heads made of granite. "Point made. But the Williams boys aren't manipulative. Stacy wants to wear the pants in the family."

"Most little girls her age are bossy."

"Since when does age have anything to do with being bossy?" he teased, dropping the canvas bag to the pavement.

Taking the remark as a good-natured jibe, Joyce made certain no one was close enough to hear and asked, "Do bossy women wear lace Jockey shorts? Know where I can buy some?"

His dark eyes dropped to the mint green short-shorts he'd convinced her to wear. "Uh-huh. Lacy bikini panties fit you perfectly. If you get too big for your britches, or in this case—panties,

I'd recommend shopping at Frederick's of Hollywood."

Joyce grinned at the silent promises his eyes were making as they flickered along her curves. "Careful, Mr. Williams, or I'll have you volunteering for something that will keep you from mowing the field this afternoon."

"If that *something* means what I think it means, where do I sign on the dotted line as a permanent volunteer?"

Hearing Stacy skip across the parking lot, whistling, Joyce wondered exactly what he meant by volunteering permanently.

"Everything's cool, Uncle Ben," Stacy said, smiling. "I told Sonny it would take an hour to mow the field and then we'd come by and pick him up. Bubba said it was okay for Sonny to come over to our house for a while afterward and . . ."

Ben groaned aloud in frustration. "Stacy, dear, I told you'd I'd made other plans. I said *maybe* we would go to the batting cages."

"Yeah," Stacy agreed, bobbing her head up and down, "you and Joyce, and Sonny and me— we, meaning more than one person."

"That isn't what I meant and you know it," Ben protested, feeling trapped.

"Just you and me are going?"

Joyce wondered if Stacy wanted to exclude her, or if she was going to become the negotiating tool to get Ben to take Sonny along, too. Both of them

117

were assuming she'd mindlessly agree to do whatever they decided.

"Well, since Joyce is helping us do the work, I think we ought to include her in our plans."

"That's not fair, Uncle Ben. I would've asked Sonny to help, but you didn't tell me that he had to work or be left out."

"Children," Ben muttered in a bewildered tone, wondering how her childish logic worked; why it made him feel lower than a snake's belly.

"Grownups," Stacy countered, her brow puckered with perplexity.

"I'm not going to let her manipulate me." His thumb pointed back at himself. "I'm the boss in my household."

Stacy grimaced. "I told you he was bossy."

"Stubborn, both of you," Joyce said, refusing to get embroiled in their family tiff. "I'm going to start working on the field."

They wanted her to mediate the disagreement. Ben expected her to side with him because it would mean their being together. Stacy expected her to side with her because additional batting practice would improve the team's chance of winning. What they'd forgotten to consider were her wishes.

Halfway peeved at their assumption that she'd tag along whatever they decided, she removed the fire-ant killer from the backseat, and jogged to the outfield.

"Hey, wait a minute," Ben called. "We should mow the grass first."

Stacy pulled on Ben's shirttail when he started to jerk the lawn mower from the back of the vehicle. "Are you going to take us to the batting cages or not?"

Lifting the mower to the pavement, he pushed it toward the baseball diamond. "We'll see."

Please, Uncle Ben," Stacy begged.

Ben yanked on the cord to start the engine; it caught, drowning Stacy's pleas. He was wise to his niece's tactics. While he considered three different things at one time, she honed in on one goal.

"We'll see how long it takes to get the work finished. You get the weed-whip and edge around the backstop and the dugout," he shouted over the roar of the engine.

He cut an eighteen-inch path directly toward Joyce. She heard him coming. Without a glance over her shoulder, she moved to center field, then directly behind second base, broadcasting ant killer when necessary.

"Joyce!"

Deaf to his shout, she zigzagged to the left and right.

"Joyce!" Ben left the lawn mower running, but sprinted after her. "Joyce!"

Turning, she pretended to have just heard him call. "Yes?"

Sweat poured into his eyes, making them sting.

119

Irritated with Stacy and the maddening chase Joyce had led, he stormed, "Why the hell didn't you stop?"

Joyce blandly surveyed his erratic mowing. Being a mathematician, he should have cut the grass in nice little squares. The corners of her lips threatened to sweep upward. "I figured you had some new system devised to stunt the growth of grass."

"Are you trying to be funny?" he roared. "Stacy is eight. I expect her to act like a child, but you, you're a woman, dammit!"

Ben, the previously calm, cool-headed mathematician, losing his temper was a sight to behold. His dark eyes had rounded to the size of saucers. Feet spread, face beet red, his hands gesticulating wildly, he looked explosive.

She laughed boisterously when the lawn mower stalled, but he continued shouting. Shaking her head negatively, she covered her mouth. "Your male ego is showing," she taunted, pointing toward the hem of his shorts.

Automatically following the course of her finger, he looked downward. Realizing he'd lost his temper for little or no reason, he grinned self-consciously.

"You'd better calm down or you'll have a heat stroke," Joyce commented, raising her face to the hot Texas sun.

"I'm unaccustomed to chasing women around baseball fields with a lawn mower."

"Chasing women—period?"

Wiping the perspiration from his brow, he grinned. "You have to admit, it's much easier being chased than chasing."

"Is that a hint? You think I should chase after you?" Dumbfounded by his suggestion, she tossed insect poison beside his worn sneakers to give him an idea of what she thought of chasing after a man.

"I don't mind taking responsibility for doing the chasing." His eyes gleamed with contained mirth. "But responsibility is directly linked to management."

Joyce followed his Socrates-like logic. "And you're taking the responsibility for our relationship, therefore . . ."

"I'm the manager—the boss."

"Your logic is flawed, Mr. Mathematician," Joyce replied loftily. "I have living proof."

"What's that?"

"Stacy."

CHAPTER SEVEN

"Stacy?" Mentally Ben tallied up the clues Joyce had given him as to the reason for weaving across the baseball field. "She's my responsibility, but I have to fight to be her boss."

"You love her . . ." she blurted, silently adding, *but not me.* Certain he'd see the flaw she'd found in their relationship, but leaving no room for doubt, she explained in terms he'd understand, "Love is as important as zero is in a base ten numerical system. Zero is the place holder. Without six zeros a million is reduced to one. You left the zeros out of our equation."

Grinning, he cleverly twisted her meaning. "Yeah, I see what you mean. I'd love to be Stacy's boss and she won't let me."

"You'd love being my boss, but I'm not going to let you, either. When I finish here, I'm going home and dive into the pool."

"You're deserting me in my hour of need," Ben protested. "You'd force me to take Stacy and Sonny to the batting cages—without you?"

"No force." Her eyes leveled with his. "And, no invitation. I'm not going to chase you, nor are you going to take for granted that I'll tag along."

"Is that why you're upset? You think I spent the night with you and now I'm taking you for granted?"

Patting his cheek, Joyce replied, "Have fun with the two kids."

"That's a rotten way to even the score." He grabbed her wrist, determined to keep her with him. "You're going with us. One for all and all for one. Team spirit, rah, rah, rah."

Her blond eyebrow arched in disbelief. "Oh?"

"Oh," he mimicked. "Admit it. You'd rather be with us than home alone."

"What makes you think I'll be alone?" His inflated arrogance needed a severe pin pricking. Did he think after one night she would forever be at his beck and call? "We haven't discussed my plans for today. I may be having a pool party with ten thousand gorgeous hunks."

"Four zeros in ten thousand. You've forgotten that zero can also represent nothing." Ben grinned. "Should I be jealous of gorgeous hunks that mean nothing to you?"

Putting her own interpretation on his refusing to swing at a low, outside curve, Joyce concluded that he wasn't jealous because he didn't care. If he'd told her he planned on spending the afternoon with ten thousand bathing beauties, she would have arrived at the pool with a concrete baseball bat.

She refused to let him see how his lack of interest bothered her. "You're going to run out of gas before you get the field mowed," she commented, pointing to the lawn mower.

"I have an extra tank," Ben assured her. "You're absolutely dead set against going with us?"

Joyce wanted to follow him to the ends of the earth. Right onto the football field—with him being the star quarterback calling all the plays? Not a chance, she silently vowed.

"No, thanks." Her eyes glittered defiantly as they met his. He loved Stacy. That's why he might dig his heels in to keep Stacy from pushing him around, but his love for the little girl gave Stacy the advantage. "Incidentally, you're standing in a bed of ants."

He'd been so intent on getting Joyce to change her mind, he hadn't noticed. Fire ants have an uncanny knack of being able to get to their victims' knees without them knowing it. They signaled in unison *"get 'em!"*

Ben jumped backward, dusting his hands over the beastly little insects. A string of invectives regarding their size and ancestry coursed through his lips. While he ineffectively slapped at his legs, they stung.

Sympathetic to his plight, Joyce yanked the sweat towel from her belt loop, circled behind

124

him, and brushed the back of his legs. Fire ants were the scourge of the South.

"Better watch where you step," Joyce said, shaking the towel, inspecting it, then tucking it back in her belt loop. She picked up her sack of ant poison and distributed a generous application for the inhabitants of the mound where Ben had been standing.

"You, too," Ben replied, giving her words ominous meaning.

Spinning on his heel, Ben strode to the machine. Figuratively, Joyce had walked all over his male ego. He had two reasons for taking Stacy and Sonny to the batting cages. One, while the kids were occupied, he planned on devoting his attention to Joyce. And two, afterward . . . Ben's sketchy amorous plans for the late evening withered.

Damn, she's stubborn.

Damn, he's stubborn, Joyce fumed. He'd refused to ask her what she wanted to do. Dictatorially, he'd made the decision and included her. Well, she silently huffed, I'll lock myself in a padded cell before I'm crazy enough to let him schedule my life.

"Joyce?"

A tap, tap, tap on the window, and someone calling her name woke her. Uncovering her head from the pillow, Joyce cocked her ear toward the bedroom window. She'd spent the evening waiting hopefully for a phone call. Disappointed, she gone to bed. Dreams had to be better than reality.

Midnight? She turned on the bedside lamp. One glance at the clock had her kicking off the covers and dashing to the window. She raised it halfway and saw Ben sitting in a rocking chair he'd taken from the front porch.

"Ben! What are you doing here?"

"Following an old Italian custom—Texas style."

She pushed her braided hair back over her shoulder. "Don't you know how dangerous it is to sneak around outside someone's house? Texans shoot first and ask questions later." Her threat bounced ineffectively off his engaging smile. "Okay. You're safe. Come around to the front door and I'll let you in."

"Uh-uh." He strummed the guitar in lap. "I'm serenading my sweetheart."

Her eyes lit with pleasure. She couldn't believe her ears. Ben's agile fingers stroked the strings with as much expertise as he'd had when touching her. She sank to her knees, heart pounding, propping her elbows on the window and her chin in her hands.

At first, he hummed the melody, then he sang the words to a ballad she'd never heard. His telephone voice the first night she'd spoken to him had intrigued her; his mellow seductive singing sent shivers down her spine.

His ballad told the story of a notoriously wild

bandit, Tex, charmed by a prim and proper "good" woman, sweet Jenny. Although he loved her passionately, the long arm of the law separated them. While hiding in the hills, she came to him and surrendered her innocence. Afterward, she cried out her fears. Tex returned to the safety of her home. Unable to dry the memory of her tears from his skin, the desperado surrendered to the sheriff. Yearning, waiting, longing, Tex counted the days until he'd climb the steps to the hangman's noose. In the midst of a cloudburst, sweet Jenny saved him and they thundered off into the desert never to be seen again. Rain, like true love, is scarce in the desert. But when rain falls from the heavens, flowers grow wild and free on the hillsides. They're known by Texans as Sweet Jenny.

Joyce sighed as the mournful strains of the last minor chord echoed into darkness.

"Beautiful," she whispered, entranced by the tale of the star-crossed lovers.

Setting the guitar aside, Ben leaned toward her, placing his hand on the screen. Mesmerized by the emotion behind his music, Joyce raised her hand, touching his.

"We need to talk," Ben said, a wistful note lingering in his voice. "Unlatch the screen."

"Come around to the front door."

"Now who's being practical? Haven't you ever fantasized about having your lover climb up a rose trellis to your balcony?"

There were times when Ben's astuteness made her wonder if he'd been inside her head, reading her thoughts. What high school girl hadn't romanticized after reading *Romeo and Juliet* in English class?

She unlatched the wooden screen and pushed it outward. Ben lithely stepped over the windowsill, holding the screen with one hand to keep it from banging, and his guitar in the other.

Her bedroom suddenly seemed smaller. The bedside lamp cast long shadows in the corners of the room. Darkness invited intimacy. Her eyes darted to her tousled bed; her hands fluttered aimlessly as though smoothing the sheets into respectable orderliness.

Without realizing what she was doing, she moved backward until her knees touched the mattress. Ben Williams had the damnedest effect on her. She had the distinct feeling the wildflowers in Texas wouldn't bloom again unless she held out her arms to him.

Ben propped his guitar against the wall. In the dappled moonlight, his eyes raked over her frilly, short nightgown. Pert little bows, that he knew could be disposed of with a mere flick of his fingers, held the gown at her shoulders. He wondered how she could appear innocent and seductive, both at the same time.

He shoved his hands deep into the pockets of his slacks. They knotted into tight fists. He'd come to talk, he sternly reminded himself.

"You should have stuck around this afternoon. Sonny rode his bike to the ball diamond. I practiced pitching while the kids batted." Ben concentrated on keeping his eyes on a dark corner beyond Joyce's back. "We didn't go to the batting cage after all." He paused, gathering his thoughts. "You left because you thought I'd put Stacy's plans ahead of yours. Right?"

"Partially."

"Stacy depends on me; she's a major part of my life. I may growl and gripe—while she affectionately calls me a mean ol' sidewinder, but we love each other. I'm all the family she has."

Ben wasn't telling Joyce anything she hadn't already surmised. She wasn't jealous of Stacy. Competing with a child for Ben's time and affection would be childish.

"You're Stacy's father figure. I don't begrudge the love you two share."

She heard his sigh of relief. Whatever problems they had, he was glad Stacy wasn't one of them.

"You didn't like the idea of taking the kids somewhere?"

"That wasn't the problem."

"Then why did you hightail it out of there? Something displeased you."

Pulling hen's teeth was easier than getting her to explain where he'd gone wrong. He seldom had to justify his actions; he rarely compromised. And yet with Joyce he found himself wanting to

129

cooperate. Satisfying only Stacy and himself left him feeling strangely empty.

"I wasn't consulted," she answered bluntly. Her hands fluttered to her breasts, unintentionally drawing his attention to their full lushness. "You were put out with Stacy for making plans without telling you, but it was perfectly all right for you to plan my afternoon without asking me."

Ben had a difficult time countering her claim. He'd been thoughtless. Much as he admired her independent spirit, he silently admitted to deriving pleasure from having her bend to his will. At the moment, he'd have liked nothing better than to coax her backward onto the bed and feel her tremble beneath his hands. He focused his eyes to the left of her to keep himself under tight control. They couldn't settle anything in bed.

"Stacy and I have a running feud. Sometimes I joke about being a benign dictator." The explanation was weak. Joyce wasn't his ward, nor was she a child. He felt his fingernails digging into the palm of his hands. He owed her an apology, but damn, her prolonged silences weren't making it easy.

Aware of the darkness, of being in her bedroom, of how she was pushing him away when she wanted to draw him close, made her rely on her wit. She had difficulty sounding flippant and cool when hot blood coursed through her veins. Memories of the last time he'd been in her bedroom clouded her determination to stand firm. The open rebellion presently taking place was in her mind. Her body knew exactly how to compromise—and love it.

Ben cocked his head to one side and thrust his jaw forward. "Okay. Punch me."

"What?" she asked, stupefied by his command.

"Punch me." He stepped forward until he was within easy reach. "You're the physical one around here. Get it out of your system. Knock some sense into my head."

Joyce tried, but she couldn't help but grin. Her toes tingled as she felt his foot nudge hers apart. Her chest tightened, eager for his touch. "Don't be ridiculous. I haven't hit anybody since I was in second grade."

"I'd rather be punched than exiled from grace," he teased.

Looping her arms across his shoulders, she asked, "Why don't you try a simple apology?"

"Something like, Joyce MacIntyre, I humbly beg you to forgive me for being an arrogant ass?"

"Yeah. You've got the idea." She inched forward until her lips could barely touch his jaw. The slight stubble on his chin contrasted beautifully with the sleek softness of his hair. "Why don't you ask me if I have plans for the wee hours of the morning?"

"Joyce," he repeated, "what are your plans for the wee hours of the morning?"

"None that can't be"—she glanced over her

shoulder at the empty, mussed bed—"re-arranged."

Ben groaned and cradled her hip to hip, thigh to thigh. "I'd like nothing better than to let my head make a dent on the pillow next to yours, but . . ." His lips dusted her forehead and cheeks. "Stacy is home by herself. I've got to . . . go."

His lips took hers with frustrated fierceness. Responsibility for Stacy's care and his driving desire for Joyce fought for supremacy. His hand trailed across her shoulder and plucked at the tiny bow. Her nightgown was as accommodating as her parted lips; it slid below her breast.

Her head was swimming. The hard thrust of his tongue, his hips arching toward her, silently communicated how much he needed her. She could easily draw him into her bed and keep him there until the sun rose.

"You can't leave Stacy alone all night," she huskily whispered against his lips.

"I know." His lips nibbled her ear and neck, igniting fires as they lowered to the sensitive hollow at the base of her neck. She tasted of moonlight and flowers, a heady intoxicant, one he could become addicted to.

Irresponsibility tempted him; passion recklessly percolated through him. Each love bite resonated with urgency. Dare he stay? Stacy slept heavily, but occasionally she'd wake up to get a drink of water. Brave as she was, she'd panic if

132

she found herself alone in a dark, empty house. He had to leave . . . now.

As though they had both come to the same decision, her arms unwound from his neck as he released her.

"This is hell," Ben said between short breaths. "I can't stay and I can't take you home . . . can't sleep here and won't sleep there."

Feeling herself caught in his dilemma, Joyce couldn't think of a quick solution. His climbing in and out of her window for nocturnal visits had romantic appeal, but lacked the substance needed in a meaningful relationship.

A thin slice of his life wouldn't be enough.

"It's a problem," she agreed wholeheartedly.

"Yeah." Ben shook his head, pushing his forelock from his brow. "One and one makes three."

"Stacy isn't a problem for me. I think she's adorable."

"And she thinks you're *awesome.*"

"So?"

"She'd raise holy hell if I tarnished your halo by sharing my bed with you."

"Little girls are a bit Victorian," Joyce admitted. She retied the bow on her nightgown. "In all honesty, I'm opposed to live-in relationships, too. That's fine for other women, but not for me."

"You're too independent?"

"Perhaps," she replied thoughtfully. Stacy's attitudes stemmed from what Ben had taught her. Similarly, Joyce was influenced by her dad's old-fashioned cliché: Why buy the cow when the milk is free? She'd updated the idea and related it to sports. She'd give Ben and Stacy a loving cup full of love and affection. Why settle for a life decorated with red and yellow ribbons? Blue ribbons, first place in their hearts, that's what she wanted. Why accept less?

"Afraid I'll discover that I don't have a chance if you and Stacy team up against me?"

She heard his low chuckle, but Joyce realized there was a thin layer of truth underlying his wisecrack. "One pair of trousers for the three of us would be a tight fit."

"A real seam splitter."

"And I'm lousy with a needle and thread."

Ben suavely lifted her hand to his lips. "I can solve that problem," he promised. Turning her hand over, he traced her love line with the tip of his tongue, sealed it with a kiss, and folded her fingers over the kiss. "Stacy can wear the pants . . . while you and I are naked in the bedroom."

"That's certainly an impractical solution coming from a math major," she replied, loving the idea.

He walked her toward the window. "Practical men don't sing love songs in a rocking chair."

"Don't forget your guitar," she reminded, pushing the screen outward.

Moonlight lit his chiseled features as he lowered his mouth to hers for one last kiss. "G'night."

He stepped backward over the window lash. His eyes lingered on her as she leaned against the window frame. Much as he was tempted to stay, he couldn't prolong his departure. With a quick twist, he sidestepped from beneath the screen.

Joyce stood at the window long moments after she lost sight of him and could no longer hear the soft strumming of his guitar. She hooked the screen, closed the window, then hugged herself and lazily crossed to her bed.

With all her heart, she wished he could have stayed longer. Forever. But she had to respect Ben for putting what he wanted behind doing what was right. Had he been selfish or immature, he would have rationalized until he could have justified leaving Stacy at home alone. Ben held himself accountable for his actions.

Humming the ballad he'd sung, she smiled, cuddling the pillow he'd slept on the night before to her chest. A hint of his fragrance made her nose twitch. She inhaled deeply. Confident they'd find a solution to their problem she drifted into dreams filled with wildflowers and happy endings.

CHAPTER EIGHT

The next morning, before the coffee had finished perking, Joyce had three phone calls from parents of players assigned to the outfield.

"Everybody can't play in the infield," she grumped, pouring herself a cup of coffee and settling into a dinette chair. "Does Jose Cruz's mother call the Houston Astros' manager and gripe? Hell, no! He probably makes more than some of the infielders."

Glaring at the phone, she dared it to ring.

It did.

"Hello!" she greeted in a nasty tone of voice.

"Ms. MacIntyre? Joyce? My name is Don Gifford. I'm calling in regard to my son, Joey, being assigned to the outfield."

"Yes." She clenched the receiver in her hand to keep from throwing it against the kitchen wall. By now, she could recite what the caller would say. She wondered if the team mother had distributed manuscripts for irate parents to memorize.

"Joey is improving, isn't he?"

That was a double-edged question if she'd ever heard one. If she replied yes, then the father would ask her why Joey wasn't assigned to the infield. If she answered no, then the father would ask what they were doing at practices. Purely a no-win question.

"Joey's skills are improving, however . . ."

"Then shouldn't he be rewarded?"

One more interruption, Joyce mused, knowing the caller's tactic was typical of a man set on dominating the conversation, and I'll get my coaches' whistle and blast his eardrum!

"As I was saying," Joyce continued with a calmness she struggled to maintain, "Joey started the practices unable to put his glove on properly. It's his first year playing ball. There are other children . . ."

"Coaches' kids. Right?"

Joyce ground her back molars together. He'd deviated from the manuscript and interrupted her twice. A red-hot flare of temper honed her tongue to a razor-sharp edge.

"There are six infield positions and two children related to the coaches. Those two children are *not* assigned to all six positions."

"Hmph! I hear one of the coaches' kids is a girl."

Counting to ten slowly, Joyce thought the top of her head would explode. Coaching a baseball team was one helluva lot different than coaching

137

gymnastics. Parental involvement was the main difference. The parent presently deriding her hadn't stepped foot on the baseball field.

"Stacy Williams is temporarily assigned to the shortstop position."

Her teeth clamped shut between each word. She wished Ben could listen to this conversation. No, on second thought, she didn't. Ben would put Stacy in the outfield rather than have the parents think Stacy was receiving preferential treatment.

"Oh, yeah?"

"Yes, sir."

"Bubba would've put her in the outfield."

Joyce bit her tongue to keep from telling him that Stacy's fielding surpassed Bubba's son's. Sonny could outhit Stacy, but otherwise she could run circles around him. Discussing the pros and cons of each player wouldn't solve this father's problem. He wanted Joey assigned to the infield. Period.

"Joey's grandparents are going to be at the opening game."

"I'm certain they'll enjoy it."

"Not if their grandson is in the outfield," Don protested. "Especially when they see a girl playing shortstop."

Patience, Joyce reminded herself. Use logic, not anger. Put the monkey on his back.

"The assignments are temporary. How much

time are you or your wife spending practicing with Joey?"

"Surely Joey practicing three times a week with you is sufficient. With homework and other school activities, Joey is too busy."

That's a switch, Joyce mused. Usually the parents are too busy.

"Next week, Joey will be on summer vacation. Between now and the opening game, why don't you come to the scheduled practices? Sometimes a child excels when his father or mother is there."

"I work."

"Come late."

"Well, . . ."

"From six to six-fifteen, I'll reschedule the batting practice for Joey and change it to field practice. Then you'll be able to see what skills he hasn't perfected."

"Well . . ."

Joyce could hear him crawfishing. It was one thing to badger the team manager, but another thing to be recruited into watching his child practice.

"Yes?"

"I wouldn't want you to have to reschedule activities just for my child."

"No problem."

"Joey shouldn't miss batting practice with his teammates."

"He won't. Six players rotate into the outfield position during a game. I'll have those children start with batting practice and end with fielding practice."

"I don't want Joey segregated from the better players. He learns from watching them."

Exasperated, Joyce asked, "Mr. Gifford, bottom line, what do you want?"

"I want Joey to play first base at the opening game so his grandparents will be proud of him." His voice raised until he was shouting.

"Yelling at me won't improve Joey's skills. You've forgotten a few essential facts. Baseball is a team sport with nine positions. All the children can't play first base."

"Well, you don't have to get nasty. If you were a man, I'd . . ."

Joyce refused to be bullied or threatened. She'd tried reason, being politely cordial, and giving helpful hints. This man had rejected all three. She silently counted to ten and recited the alphabet. Enough was enough. He had her so mad she felt certain she could bend a baseball bat with her bare hands.

"Mr. Gifford, I'm going to manage this team fairly. You've insulted my integrity, tried to intimidate me, and now you're threatening me with violence. Mister, my address is next to my phone number on the team directory. You do what you think is right! Good-bye!"

She disconnected the line without waiting for a reply.

In the privacy of her home, she did something

she'd never do in public. She raised her fists toward the ceiling, stomped both feet on the floor
and screamed in frustration.

The phone rang, cutting her wail in half.

"Don't you dare!" she warned the phone, certain Don Gifford wanted the last word. She
pointed at the phone as though the person on the
other end of the line could hear her without her
lifting the receiver. "So help me, Mr. Gifford, I'll
find your address and personally deliver the entire contents of the manager's kit on your doorstep. *You* manage a team with nine kids playing
first base!"

The phone continued ringing.

If that man had the gall to call her again, she
wasn't going to hold back. She'd give it to him
straight—with both barrels loaded. Eyes shooting
angry sparks, she jerked the receiver from the
cradle.

"Don't you dare say another word," Joyce
blasted before Don could get a word in edgewise.
"I'm not going to give you the satisfaction of
quitting. You get off your duff and play ball with
your son if you want him on first base."

Joyce took a deep breath, mentally reloading
her shotgun with another round of ammunition,
and waited for Don to return fire with a macho
reply.

"G'morning, sweetheart."

Jaw dropping, she held the phone away from
her ear and stared at it. Only one man had a voice

that flowed through the telephone wires like warm honey: Ben Williams. She paused long enough to decide whether or not to unload her problems on him.

"No, it hasn't been a good morning," she said in a deflated tone. "I've had four out of the six fathers of outfielders call me. It definitely hasn't been a good morning!"

Gauging from the stinging tone of her voice, Ben knew she'd been on the wrong end of some hard line drives—and fielded them bare-handed. He wouldn't tolerate anyone abusing Joyce.

"I'll take care of it." He pulled a scratch pad from the desk drawer. "Give me their names and numbers."

With a stiff upper lip, she refused. "Your calling them isn't necessary. I can fight my own battles."

"Don't be stubborn. Tell me who called. I'll look the numbers up myself."

"Please, Ben. I don't want to argue with you unless you want Stacy switched to first base."

"Is that what the calls were about? Everybody wants their kid to play first base?"

"That's it. We're going to have the tightest infield in the league. Four players covering first."

Ben laughed. "At least you haven't lost your sense of humor."

"That's the only thing keeping me sane this morning." She made a face after taking a sip of

142

cold coffee. Two minutes ago she could have held the cup in her hand and watched it boil.

"Are you certain you don't want me to talk to them in a language they'll understand?"

"I tried logic. It didn't work."

"Logic? Too cerebral an approach. It won't break the language barrier between a female manager and a dad's pride concerning his son."

"What do you suggest?"

"Oh, I'd say something like—don't mess with my woman, for starters," he teased. "If that doesn't appeal to their he-man attitudes, I'll take a page from your book and threaten to rearrange their teeth with a baseball bat."

Her heart fluttered as she wondered how Don Gifford would have reacted to Ben's approach. Much as the second part of his idea appealed to her, she rejected it. She could not allow herself to hide behind Ben's muscles. She was the manager; she'd deal with the irate parents.

Along those same lines, she realized Ben *might* get physical should Don accuse Stacy of receiving special treatment because she was a coach's niece. She had protected Ben and Stacy as vehemently as he wanted to protect her. No, she couldn't allow Ben to interfere.

"Your woman?" she quoted, singling out the important phrase to divert his intentions.

"Yep," he drawled in true Texas fashion. "It's being announced at the opening ceremonies.

You're being introduced as Joyce MacIntyre, manager of the Astros, Ben Williams's woman."

"You'll ruin my old-maid, schoolmarm reputation," she warned. "I'll probably be fired."

"Good."

"Good? You won't think that's good when I go to Gilley's and get a job as a saloon girl," she bantered.

"Gilley's doesn't have saloon girls. You'll be destitute. The banker will knock at your door with the foreclosure papers; I'll ride up in my Cherokee and save you."

"A modern version of the ballad you sang last night?"

"Yep."

"Sorry, but the house is paid for and I'm a stockholder in the bank."

Ben groaned. "You just ruined a perfect ballad. My country and western songwriter's career went kaput!" His laughter dwindled to a low, sultry pitch. "How'd you like to invite a down-and-out songwriter to your place for dinner, Moneybags?"

"Oh, I think I can afford another can of pork 'n' beans. Am I inviting Stacy also?"

"And Priscilla. I figured it out with pencil and paper. I know exactly how many kisses I can steal while those two are dunking each other."

"How many?"

"Nope, I'm not telling. You'll have to count them one at a time."

144

"Hmm. You aren't planning on having the grand tally announced at the opening game, are you?"

"Kiss and tell? Please, a southern gentleman doesn't . . ."

"Make announcements," she completed. "What time am I inviting you over for a swim and dinner?"

"Stacy is packing up the swim gear now."

Joyce grinned. "Are southern gentlemen always this presumptuous?"

"Only when they have a niece poking them in the ribs with a toy gun while she calls them a mean ol' sidewinder. Hang on a second."

She could hear Ben telling Stacy and Priscilla the plans. Without being there, Joyce knew from the squeals that the girls were jumping up and down, hugging each other.

"No rest for the wicked. They've dashed over to Priscilla's house to get her suit. Stacy told me they'd wait for me in the car. Can I bring anything? Hot dogs? Ice? Potato chips?"

"No, thanks. I have an emergency ration in the refrigerator for unemployed songwriters." Reluctant to end the conversation but eager for him to arrive, she said, "See you soon. Oh, wait a minute. There is something you can bring—your guitar."

"See you!"

The frown she'd been wearing all morning inverted in a sunny smile. Ben and the kids had more or less invited themselves over, but what the hell. Strong hints were better than appearing at the door saying, "Here I am. Feed me. Entertain me." Anyone with a pool in their backyard has been similarly greeted.

Leisurely pouring herself another cup of coffee, Joyce felt ready for the next phone call. You want your child on first base? she mused. Why not? I'm the one who preaches the fun and games philosophy. Who cares if we win? We'll have a few chuckles, learn a smattering about the rules, swing the bat—who cares?

Sipping the scalding-hot coffee, an answer came straight from her competitive heart.

I care!

Otherwise, what difference would it make who played first? The whole team could huddle around first, then goose-step in unison to second, third, and home plate . . . if she really didn't care about winning.

Reflexively, she covered her mouth as though every parent on the team would be privy to her silent thoughts. For a woman who boasted that she knew who and what she was and where she was going, she'd forgotten several important instances in her background.

From early childhood, she'd had a burning desire to win. At six years of age, she'd smacked a classmate in the mouth because the girl had cheated while playing jacks. Her father warming her tail end had put a halt to the violence, but not to the determination to be first in everything.

She remembered the pain and frustration of discovering there were children who could run faster, swing harder, throw farther. But that spurred her to practice harder. She used her brains and her athletic ability. Nothing she'd done was illegal or could classified as poor sportsmanship. If she couldn't strike a batter out by throwing faster than a speeding bullet, she psyched the batter by her aggressive stance, by curling her lip . . . Joyce grimaced at the tactics she'd used.

She hated losing. Second-place teams didn't get a trophy for a solid reason: They lost too often.

She'd asked Don Gifford what the bottom line was for him. He wanted his child to play first base so Joey's grandparents would be proud of him. Was that so awful? Most parents wanted to be able to brag about their kids.

Irritated with herself, Joyce picked up her cup and began to pace.

Why not rotate the kids into the various fielding positions? Let each one of them have the thrill of telling their mom and dad, "Hey! I get to play first at the next game!" Wouldn't they love playing baseball more? Wouldn't they learn more? Wouldn't it be more fun for them?

She'd been the one who told the parents at the first practice that the kids were there to learn to love the game, to have fun. And yet, four players were dissatisfied—before the season opened. Fun and games had become serious business.

"I'll change everything," she muttered, setting her cup on the counter and moving to her desk. "I'll ask the kids who wants to play what position. Let them sign up for certain games. At the practices before the games, the children will have a chance to learn where to throw the ball . . . should they catch it."

Chuckling, she slid into the desk chair and sorted through the drawer until she found twelve different-colored pencils and fifteen blank sheets of white paper. "One color for each child; one sheet for each game."

Another side benefit she thought of made her toss her head back and bubble with laughter. "This little innovative plan of mine is going to blow Bubba away."

From Bubba's viewpoint, she'd be committing the equivalent of baseball suicide. The chances of the Astros winning would be slim with the best players positioned where the ball would be least likely to hit.

Merrily humming, she began making charts. She could hardly wait to tell Ben about the switch in game strategy. He'd love it!

Less than an hour later, she greeted Ben and the kids with a terrific smile and a warm hug for each of them. Both girls wore saucy, shocking-pink polka-dotted swimsuits, but Joyce could barely take her eyes from Ben's Hawaiian print trunks and shirt.

"You're staring," Ben teased unmercifully. "Stacy picked them out."

"They're . . . stunning."

Ben winked lazily. "Not what a stick-in-the-mud mathematician should wear?"

"It's certainly more conservative than what you wore the last time you went swimming here," Joyce quipped, grinning cheekily.

"Where's the pool?" Stacy asked, skipping from room to room. "Can we swim before lunch so we don't have to wait an hour?"

"Stacy!" Ben reprimanded. "Where are your manners?"

"Sorry." She didn't look the least bit contrite with her flippers slung over her shoulder and a big beach ball clasped against her waist. "You don't want us to listen to grownup talk forever and ever, do you? Where's your swim suit, Joyce? Aren't you going to swim with us?" Stacy took a quick breath and added, "You can help us dunk Uncle Ben."

Holding both hands up for silence, she answered, "You can swim right away. I have to put my suit on. Yes, I'm going to swim. No, I won't help you dunk Uncle Ben. Now it's my turn. Can you swim the length of a big pool?"

"Of course! We both took lessons!"

Joyce glanced at Ben for confirmation. He nodded.

"Go through that door." She pointed over her shoulder. "We'll be there in a little bit."

Both girls scurried through the room and out the door before the adults could change their minds.

"Whew! She can almost talk faster than she can run, can't she?" Joyce asked, stepping into Ben's open arms.

"Fast talkers run in the Williams family," Ben answered.

Joyce pulled his head down for a quick kiss. "I've got something wonderful to show you."

"Oh, yeah?" His brows wiggled comically in a poor imitation of a wicked leer.

"You're as frisky as Stacy." She took him by the hand and led him into the kitchen. "I had this brilliant idea for the team."

"Whoa! You lost me. Isn't the something wonderful you have to show me that nubile body of yours getting into a skimpy swimsuit?"

"Ben!" She imitated his exact tone when he'd chastised Stacy for poor manners. "Don't you want to hear my idea?"

"Later." His arms wrapped around her waist. "Much later."

"But . . ." Her lips were sealed by his. What the hell—baseball could wait until later. Eyes fluttering closed, she put as much enthusiasm into her kiss as she felt about her new plan.

"Mmm. I've been waiting hours for that. Now I'll be able to make it through the day."

"On one kiss?"

"I'm testing my won't power."

"Don't you mean will power?" she asked, peppering his cheeks with tiny kisses.

"Oh, sweetheart, my will power is working overtime. I'm more than willing. It's my won't power that blows a fuse every time I see you. On the drive over here, I told myself that I won't remember the last time in the pool. I won't touch you as often as I'd like. I won't . . ."

Joyce laughed. "I get the picture. My won't power is weakening, too."

"The kids could come running in here at any moment." He firmly took her by the shoulders. His won't power failed. He pulled her back into his arms and stole another kiss. "After last night, I won't start anything we can't finish. Go get your suit on and I'll meet you at the pool. Both girls can swim, but I like to keep an eye on them."

"I'll hurry. Why don't you light the grill. I'll bring the hot dogs, buns, and chips."

"Need help carrying anything?"

"Nope. I'm organized."

Ben playfully swatted her rear end. "Like every good Little League manager should be. Everything planned to the nth degree."

"Let go of me. You're on your way to check on the girls, remember?" she said, paying him back for the spank by leaning backward against his arms and rocking from side to side against him.

151

"I can't . . . can . . . won't . . . will . . ." He changed his mind with each brush of her hips. ". . . *will* follow orders today."

His unexpected release caught Joyce off balance. Quickly recovering, she lightly poked him in the ribs. "It's about time you learned who was boss around here."

"You?"

Joyce pivoted on one foot, and giving him a sexy wink from over her shoulder, she replied drolly, "No, Ben. Stacy and Priscilla rule the roost for today. Agreed?"

Ben nodded. "I hope you know what you're asking for. Stacy and Margaret Thatcher are distant cousins."

"Oh, yeah? Maybe that explains where you get the urge to dictate policy. I just hope you're receptive to innovative ideas."

Whetting his curiosity, leaving him wanting an explanation, Joyce sashayed from the kitchen. While they were both in high spirits she wanted to spring her idea on him, not that she thought for a moment he would object.

Ben Williams championed the underdog and fought for what was fair for everybody. A baseball championship was unimportant to him. Her idea would prove that it was unimportant to her, too.

Glancing in the mirror, she practiced using her "won't power." "I won't take the game too seriously. I won't assign the kids to positions they don't want to play. And I won't let my driving ambition to win defeat the purpose behind Little League baseball."

CHAPTER NINE

The right time and opportunity for Joyce to present her brilliant idea to Ben took longer than she anticipated. The four of them swam, ate lunch, played croquet, swam, and barbecued dinner, without her being alone with Ben. By eight o'clock that evening, she felt as though she would burst.

Priscilla sprawled bonelessly in the backseat on the short drive to Ben's house. Happily exhausted, Stacy hunched forward, dawdling with Joyce's long ponytail. "Are you going to tuck me in?" she asked Joyce.

Ben shot Stacy a warm smile. The nightly routine had been his exclusive privilege. At bedtime, Stacy became all cuddly little girl. With a slow smile of satisfaction and a lazy wink, he gave his blessing to Stacy's request.

"If you want me to," Joyce replied.

Stacy yawned as only a child can; mouth wide open, jaw popping. "Mm-hmm."

Between the girls' unsuccessful attempts to

dunk Ben, Joyce had learned that Mrs. Shane arrived on Sunday evening and stayed until Thursday night. Promising, she'd thought, very promising. The restricting hurdle of his being a single parent was gradually diminishing.

Ben parked the car in the driveway.

"Is Priscilla asleep?" Ben asked Stacy.

Stacy put her finger over her mouth and bobbed her head.

"Joyce, I'll carry Pris over to her house if you take Stacy inside." He opened his door, then went to the back passengers' door. Joyce and Stacy grinned at each other as they each opened their doors. "Young lady," he whispered, "you brush your teeth."

"Aw, Uncle Ben, toothpaste tastes super-yukky," Stacy said, making a silly face. One stern look from her uncle changed her mind. Grudgingly she grumbled, "Okay."

Hand in hand, Joyce and Stacy walked into the house and straight to Stacy's bedroom.

"You can sit on my bed while I change into my jammies and go to the john," Stacy offered, rummaging through her bottom dresser drawer. Testing Joyce, she added, "Don't read the notes from my boyfriend that are on the nightstand."

Joyce nodded, her eyes scanning Stacy's room. For a tomboy, Stacy had a delightful mishmash of furnishings. Hanging on her ruffled canopy bedposts were baseball caps and cheerleader pom-poms. The small, gingham checked wall-

155

paper had posters of famous sports figures and statuesque ballerinas. Her dresser top held bottles of cologne, bobby pins and barrettes, and autographed baseballs and sports trophies.

It poignantly reminded Joyce of her own room when she was growing up.

Stacy opened her mouth for inspection and widely grinned as she hopped into her bed. On all fours, she gave one or two good bounces, then slithered between the sheets. Joyce watched Stacy's sleepy blue eyes take one quick glance at the undisturbed folded notebook paper on her night table. Joyce passed the privacy test.

"You can kiss me," Stacy said with a wistful note in her young voice. "Uncle Ben gives loud, smacking kisses, but I love them. Ever had a hair kiss?"

Joyce grinned. "Can't say that I have," she admitted, leaning over Stacy's scrubbed, shiny face.

She lurched forward as Stacy grabbed her around the neck, burying her nose against Stacy's flat chest. Right in front of her ponytail, she felt Stacy's lips.

"M-m-m-m," Stacy hummed, then made a loud popping sound. "I gave you a doozy of a hair kiss 'cause you're special."

Along with the hair kiss, Joyce felt a peculiar sensation in her chest. Stacy's enthusiastic kiss seemed to touch her maternal instincts and bring them to full bloom.

She raised her head and looked into the little

156

girl's cornflower-blue eyes. "I think you're a pretty neat kid yourself," she confided, stroking her bangs back on her forehead.

"Do you like me a lot?"

"Mm-hmm!"

Stacy grinned, pulling Joyce's pale blond hair forward and winding it around her small wrist. "I like you a lot, too. There aren't many people I'd share Uncle Ben with, you know."

"Oh yeah?" One eyebrow cocked in disbelief. You've told me a few stories about . . ."

"I know," she admitted. "I've been trying to fix Uncle Ben up with a whole bunch of ladies. But you're the only one that could hit a home run."

Joyce chuckled. "Is that what makes me special?"

"Yeah. And you don't walk funny, or have bad telephone manners. That's important."

Somehow Joyce got lost. She understood why Stacy thought hitting a homer was important, but walking . . . and telephone manners? Those were totally unexpected.

Stacy covered her mouth and yawned. Her eyelids drifted closed, but she held on to Joyce's hair. "Do you believe in wishes coming true? I mean, if you try real hard to be a good girl, and you make the same wish every night."

Knowing how Stacy's mind bounced from one topic to another, Joyce guessed that Stacy was referring to the baseball team. Did Stacy expect her to promise that she'd have another trophy to add to her collection?

Cautiously, she answered, "Wishes can come true, but sometimes we have to help them along by working very hard to make them come true."

"At the baseball tryouts, I wished that you'd choose me for your team, and you did. Now I'm working on another wish. I can't tell you though or it won't come true."

Joyce unwound her hair from Stacy's wrist. Feathering a kiss on the sleepy little girl's brow, she murmured, "Maybe our wish is the same."

One eye peeked open, a hint of a smile curved the bow of her lips. "That would be nice. Between the two of us, it's gonna come true."

"Tell you what. At the end of the baseball season, you tell me if your wish came true, and I'll tell you if mine came true. Okay?"

Rolling to her side, Stacy said, "Okay. G'night."

"G'night, honey. Sweet dreams."

Joyce turned out the light and tiptoed to the door. Ben was leaning against the wall, waiting.

"Were you eavesdropping on our girltalk?" she asked, wondering if he didn't trust her alone with Stacy.

"Yep."

"You know the old saying about eavesdroppers never hearing good things about themselves, don't you?"

"Yeah, but Stacy doesn't say bad things about

158

me behind my back. She's too honest. So are you." He put his hand on the small of her back and nudged her toward the family room. "Face to face, right between the eyeballs is where Stacy lands her verbal blows."

Joyce slipped her arm around his waist. "I may be on her hit list in the near future. I think she's making some pretty tall wishes about who wins the league trophy this year."

"Stacy wants to win . . . we all do."

"Winning isn't everything." Seeing the strange look come over Ben's face, she added, "I've told you that I want the kids to learn to love the game, to look forward to playing again next year."

"Now don't misunderstand me, I don't go along with Bubba's theory to win at all costs, but we both know the players on a championship team are going to sign up for the next season. Coming in last place doesn't build confidence like winning does."

Joyce worried the inner lining of her mouth. She barely noticed they were going through the kitchen until Ben asked her if she'd care for a glass of white wine. She continued toward the family room while Ben lingered in the kitchen.

"Yes, thanks."

"Make yourself at home. Curl up on the sofa and kick your shoes off. Mrs. Shane gets here around nine thirty. If you don't mind, I'll wait until she's here to take you home."

"That's fine," Joyce agreed, wondering how Ben would react to her new plan for the baseball team.

Her exuberance over her reorganization of fielding positions had been capped as tightly as a fielder caps a grounder in the web of his glove. She collapsed on the sofa and removed her sandals. Knees bent, legs folded, toes tucked behind the cushion, she contemplated dropping the whole idea.

Winning was more important to Ben than she'd previously realized.

Maybe Ben and Bubba were coaching Little League for the same reason . . . to recapture the glory they'd had as a child when they'd participated in team sports. She suspected Bubba had never been a great player. His son being one of the best players on the team gave Bubba a vicarious thrill that gave him extra satisfaction. Coaching was an ego trip for Bubba.

Her brow puckered. She'd seen Ben's trophies intermingled with Stacy's collection. Confident Ben and Bubba weren't coaching for the same reasons, she decided to find out what he thought of letting the players decide which positions they wanted to play.

"I've been thinking about making some changes in the fielding positions," she said hesitantly.

"Don't let a couple of phone calls change anything you don't feel would benefit the team. Once we're winning, they'll be in the stands rooting for the whole team instead of just their kid."

She could hear the glasses clinking together as Ben carried them into the room. Ben set the long-stemmed crystal glasses on the polished cocktail table, then filled them. Their fingers touching as Joyce took the glass, she felt a familiar shiver skitter down her spine. Susceptible to the warm glow in his eyes that had nothing whatsoever to do with baseball, she gulped down the wine to fortify herself.

Ben's facial expression changed to one of disbelief. "I didn't know you were that thirsty. Take it easy or you'll get tipsy and I'll be carrying you into your house."

When he refilled her glass, she gave him a weak grin. She seldom drank alcoholic beverages. Already she could feel the wine having a slight effect on her.

"Nobody wants to play outfield for the entire season," she said, leading into the radical changes she planned to make.

Ben sat beside her on the sofa with his wine-glass in one hand and the other resting on the back of the sofa behind Joyce's head. "The roster isn't engraved in marble. Nothing is permanent. We can change them."

Now she was getting somewhere. "Often?"

"As often as you think is necessary."

"Every game?"

"Sure. One or two changes isn't going to upset the apple cart."

Joyce sipped her wine, eyes downcast. "How about switching all the positions . . . at every game?"

Ben laughed at her preposterous joke. Her eyes raised and he realized from the icy glint in them that perhaps she wasn't pulling his leg.

"You're kidding, aren't you?"

Joyce leaned forward and put her glass on the table. She couldn't fight a major battle with one hand occupied. Ben was looking at her as though she'd just stepped off a spaceship and had weird little antennas sticking from her head.

"No," she replied quietly with firmness. "I'm not."

"Why?"

"Because every kid on the team wants to play the infield positions. And every parent in the bleachers, for numerous reasons, wants their kid on first base . . . or shortstop."

Ben heard more than what she was saying. Being perceptive, he asked, "Did one of the phone calls you fielded this morning have anything to do with the coaches' kids having the best positions?"

"Yes," she replied, without divulging the parent's name.

"Sweetheart, that's sour grapes on their part. Stacy and Sonny are two of the most capable

162

players. They would be infielders regardless of who was coaching."

"Maybe." She shrugged. "Maybe not. How would you feel if I rotated Stacy in and out of the outfield? Only allowed her to play half the game?"

"I'd think you were crazy."

"The parents who phoned this morning would agree with you."

"But Joyce, that's different," he argued. "You can't expect Stacy to run in from the outfield and cover the fumbles of the infielders."

"I don't. But look at the other side. How are these kids going to learn how to field a hit if the batters can't hit hard enough to get it out to them?"

Seeing how Ben was stumped for a reply, she pushed her advantage. "Half the team won't appreciably improve. Why excel at catching the ball when the chances are it will never come to you?"

"There's something wrong with your logic. I just can't put my finger on it." Ben sank into the cushions at the far end of the sofa. "You can't win by shuffling players around."

"I can't *lose* by shuffling them. We agreed at the beginning that the main objective of Little League is to teach the kids to love the game."

"They aren't going to love anything or anybody, especially the coaching staff, if we never win."

"How can you predict that we'll never win?"

Ben rubbed his stomach. "Right here . . . gut level I know we'll be booed off the field."

"I think you're wrong. The kids and their parents will love it."

"Hmph! I know two parents who won't."

"Bubba and who else? You?"

"Yeah, not to mention Sonny and Stacy. They've practiced hard for their positions. You're giving them away to kids who don't deserve them."

"Why don't they deserve them? Because they weren't born with the natural ability Stacy has? Because their parents don't have the time . . . or take the time to practice with them? Because . . ."

Ben motioned for her to stop. "You're making me feel like a rat for being a good parent. That doesn't make sense."

"It makes about as much sense as you assigning a kid an outfield position because he or she doesn't have 'good parents' or 'good genes.' "

"The whole idea is unorthodox. It'll never work."

Joyce rose to her feet. "A silly woman's whim?"

"Sit down. Be reasonable," Ben urged. "Bubba will quit. You'll be short a coach."

"Bubba's no prize. I disagree with almost everything the man says and does. What about you? Are you going to quit or stand behind me?"

"I told you I'm not a quitter."

She jutted her chin forward, unaware of doing it. "You've also told me you don't like standing *behind* any woman. I'm taking full responsibility for the team. Are you with me or not?"

"Joyce, sweetheart, be reasonable. I can't back you when I think what you're going to do is unreasonable."

"I am being reasonable," she said, voice flat. "I'm being consistent with the principles I believe in. You're the one being unreasonable. The only argument you've come up with has to do with winning a trophy, a hunk of gold-colored metal. What are you? A Bubba in disguise?"

"Now you're being silly."

"Don't call me silly. Unorthodox, fine . . . but not silly. What's wrong with the comparison? Bubba wants to win; you want to win. Bubba wants his kid in the infield; you want your kid in the infield. Bubba will object to the plan; you already do object to the plan. As far as baseball is concerned, show me a difference between the two of you."

"I don't stomp and yell at the kids."

"True. Maybe you should. Sonny is a better hitter than Stacy," she goaded. "Take her to the batting cages and yell at her for an hour or two. See what happens."

"One of us, me most likely, wouldn't be leaving the cage." Ben cast her a rueful grin, hoping to let humor bring levity into the conversation. His attempt fell flat.

Joyce wouldn't budge an inch, although she was tempted to return his smile. "Stacy is young, but you've taught her to stand for what she believes in. If winning isn't important, and keeping the fun and games spirit alive for these kids is important, why won't you support what I believe in?"

"I didn't say I'd quit coaching."

"That's support? Come on, Ben," she derided. "I get more support from pantyhose. I want the same kind of wholehearted commitment you give Stacy."

"No. What you want is to give the orders and for me to blindly follow them. The tone of this discussion reminds me of arguments between Stacy's parents. My brother heard the same kind of talk from his wife before he globetrotted along after her. Stacy's mother made sense, too." A bitter residue coated his tongue. "The situation you're leading me into isn't fatally dangerous, but you're using the same kind of emotional blackmail to get what you want. You're aware that I've fallen for you. You've come up with this bizarre idea and you want me to give credence to it because of how I feel about you. Sorry, but no, Joyce, I won't be led around by the nose by any woman. I made that clear from the beginning."

She flinched when she heard the grim determination in his voice. Unless she backed down, she was going to lose far more than a baseball game. Fun and games would be over for her and Ben.

Ben rose to his feet. "I'll take you home. We both need some time to think."

"What about Stacy? Mrs. Shane isn't here."

"I won't be gone long. I'll leave the lights on and note on the kitchen table. Should Stacy awaken, she'll know I'll be right back."

Her heart sank to her toes as he motioned for her to precede him to the front door. Her arguments had been infallible for letting the players choose their positions. Likewise, she couldn't fault his logic regarding his late sister-in-law.

"One and one don't make three," she muttered, holding back her tears.

"And I didn't run fast enough to keep from getting tagged out," Ben said with remorse. "Let's go."

Once they were inside the Cherokee neither of them spoke. Ben kept his eyes on the road; Joyce stared through the side window. At her house, Ben courteously escorted her to her door.

Joyce simply couldn't let a perfect day end on a sour note. "Thanks for inviting yourself over today."

"Thank you for accepting my invitation," Ben countered without a smile. "Any chance of you exercising a woman's prerogative and changing your mind?"

"About as much chance as you committing yourself to supporting me in what deep in your heart you know is fair for the kids."

Ben's hands closed around her upper arms, but

he solemnly shook his head. "You're being stubborn as a mule."

She inched toward him. Her eyes begged him to relent. "Yeah. You, too."

"It's been fun . . . while it lasted." His arms folded her against his larger frame. Never has a woman fit so beautifully, he thought, blinking to clear his blurred eyesight.

"Fun and games, right from the start." Her arms wrapped tightly around his waist; her fingers dug into his back. "We'll get over it."

Ben buried his face against her neck. "Yeah. Whatever *it* is, we'll survive."

They stood locked in each other's arms for long, long silent moments.

Ben cleared his throat. "I'm having a helluva time convincing myself I can get to my car in an upright position. I may have to crawl."

"I was wondering if I'd get any sleep tonight if I don't change the sheets on the bed." She sniffed. "The other set I own is in the laundry. I'll be up all night doing the wash."

He touched her face very gently. "I'm sorry."

Joyce didn't know if he was apologizing for the sheets or for being so damned hardheaded. She did know that unless she got inside the house within the next five seconds, she'd be bawling like a kid who'd lost her first love.

She straightened her back; she clenched her jaw to keep it from wobbling. Through tight lips, she said, "I'll see you . . ."

"Yeah." His won't power fizzled. He lightly kissed her closed lips. Once. Twice. Uncertain he'd survive a third kiss without her responding, he bounded down the steps.

Joyce slumped against the screen door. His car's taillights disappeared from sight long before she had the strength to go inside.

Tears she'd been too proud to shed in front of Ben rolled down her cheeks. She stumbled through the house to the bedroom and flung herself on the bed. Shoulders shaking, she sobbed. Her knees protectively drew to her chest. Small keening sounds came from deep inside her. Her fist pounded the pillow again and again. She hurt. Worse, she wasn't certain this hurt would ever go away.

During the return trip to his house, Ben frantically searched for the flaw in Joyce's logic. Either he coached to win or he let Joyce switch the positions around at each game like nonstop musical chairs. She was the team's manager. She had the right to make the decision . . . even when both coaches knew her decision would result in total disaster.

Logically, he decided two factors could make her change her mind. One, the kids rejected the plan. Not likely with there being more weak players on the team than strong players. Or two, after the dismal defeat the Astros would suffer at the opening game, she'd reconsider.

Ben parked his car beside Mrs. Shane's Lynx. In slow motion, he opened the car door, rolled to his feet. Like an old man, his feet shuffled as he walked to the front door.

"Ben?" Mrs. Shane called from the kitchen. "I didn't expect you home so . . ." her voice faded when she saw his compressed lips and the white brackets surrounding them. Concerned by the paleness of his face, she asked, "Are you sick? Is there anything I can do?"

Sharing his problem wouldn't solve it. "My head is pounding."

"Too much Texas sun can do that to a body. You have to be careful," she fussed. "You sit down at the table and I'll get some aspirin for you."

"I'll get them. You go on with what you were doing."

"Nonsense. I'm whipping up a dessert for tomorrow night. It can wait for a minute or two while I take care of you. How about a bite to eat?"

"I'm not hungry."

"Tired?"

"No."

He got a glass from the cupboard and filled it with tap water while she rummaged in the cupboard.

"Here you are. These will have you feeling better in no time." She dropped two tablets into his opened palm.

170

"Thanks."

Mrs. Shane closely scrutinized his face while he took the medicine. When a man wasn't hungry or tired and took aspirin for the first time since she'd known him, something dire had happened. Having raised four sons, she recognized the symptoms. Woman trouble.

"What did you and Stacy do today?"

"Went swimming."

"At the recreation center?"

"No, at the Astro manager's house." Being evasive was pointless. His housekeeper could get information out of a Russian spy. "Joyce MacIntyre's pool. We spent the day there."

"Aha." She smiled, nodding her head. "How kind of her. Now we owe her a nice dinner invitation. Steak, salad, baked potato with sour cream, and strawberry shortcake. How does she like her steak?"

"Raw."

Without a blink, Mrs. Shane asked, "Does she eat potatoes the same way? She's certainly easy to cook for."

A tired smile hovered on Ben's lips. "Don't bother. I struck out with her."

"Care to tell me about it? My boys always felt better when they told me about their love problems."

"She's come up with a crazy idea and she's being stubborn."

Mrs. Shane picked up her mixing bowl and be-

171

gan to vigorously stir the contents. "She wants a wedding ring, huh? I knew I liked her from the moment I first met her. Good, old-fashioned values. None of that live-together fol-de-rol."

"Mrs. Shane . . . she wants to let the kids choose what positions they play."

"Oh? Oh, dear, I'm not a sports fan, but I seem to recall my Johnny playing several different positions."

"At every game?"

"Well, now that you mention it, he did squat down behind the boy with the bat for an entire summer. I could hardly bare to watch." She shuddered. "Surely you aren't going to let a little disagreement over who plays what come between you."

"I gave her valid reasons as to why her idea wouldn't work. She stubbornly refused to see reason. She's exasperating. She's trying to make me go along with something that I know is wrong."

"Isn't that what the man usually does?" She darted a cherubic smile in Ben's direction. "Times have changed. Do you love her?"

"I thought I was falling in love until I realized I'd have to have my nose pierced to fit the wedding ring," Ben said sardonically. "We've had several discussions regarding who's boss."

"But Ben, you don't like a brainless, clinging-vine type of woman. You admire a woman who can make decisions and stick to them."

"Not when they conflict with my decision," Ben said grumpily.

"Oh?" She looked and sounded confused. She wasn't. "My husband always let me make the little decisions and he made the big ones."

"That's reasonable."

"I thought so. He solved the world's problems and I decided where we lived, who we associated with, and which bills to pay with his money."

Stunned by the fall into her verbal trap, Ben stared at his housekeeper as though she hadn't worked for him three years.

She covered her mouth and gave a girlish giggle. "That *was* naughty of me to poke fun at your problems. But, sometimes we do take life a bit too seriously. Life is a game. Sometimes you win; sometimes you lose. But you always lose when you forget how to laugh."

"Believe me, Stacy's ballgames are going to produce belly laughs the whole world will hear."

"My, my, maybe I'll attend a few of them. Most of them are so intense . . . so boring for the children."

"Boring? They wouldn't sign up if they thought they were going to be bored."

Mrs. Shane nodded in agreement. "That's what I thought. But look at those little kids way out in the field. They look like miniature horses, sleeping on their feet. Aren't they bored? They certainly didn't look like they were having fun to me."

Ben stood there looking dumbfounded. Twice in the same evening he'd listened to illogical reasoning and it had made sense to him. Maybe he was the one who was crazy. Tomorrow Stacy would probably think switching positions was a wonderful idea!

"I'm going to bed. Wake me up when the baseball season is over."

CHAPTER TEN

"You aren't going to quit?" Joyce repeated, unable to believe what Bubba had said.

"No way, José. This harebrained scheme of yours might work. Hell, all kids do better when they're doin' what they wanna do. It's when a parent tells 'em what to do that they go deaf."

"What if we lose?"

"We won't."

Joyce wished she felt as confident. "Coach Williams disapproves of the whole idea. He may resign."

"Ben? Don't kid yourself. He's got more stick-to-it than rice and beans clingin' to a Texan's ribs during the Great Depression. Frankly, since he's doin' the pitchin', he'll have plenty on his own plate to worry about. I've seen pitchers booed off the field by the parents."

As she spoke to Bubba, she watched the automatic pitching machine throw strike after strike.

"Stacy relayed the message that Ben had to go to Cape Canaveral on an emergency trip, but he'll be back for opening game. I'll have to take over the pitching mound until he returns."

"Hey!" Bubba shouted at Sonny, who was in the batting cage. "Choke up on your bat! Did you see that? He acts like he didn't hear me. Parent-deaf, plain and simple."

"Each team member should have had two turns. I'm going to start rounding them up." Joyce pushed away from the twenty-foot cyclone fence. "Thanks, Bubba. I appreciate your cooperation."

Bubba grinned. "If this scheme of yours fails, I'm gonna get a job on the first shrimping boat headed for China."

"Save me a place on the oars," Joyce replied. "Saturday is the big day, opening ceremonies, and then our first game. I'll see about some kind of coach's shirt for you."

"My wife took care of that. Want her to make somethin' for you?"

"No. I'll wear a T-shirt left over from the gymnastic tournaments that has MANAGER on the back. See you Thursday."

"Yeah. Five . . . sharp."

Joyce blew her whistle. Players who'd finished batting came running. "You ride in the car you came in. See you . . ."

"THURSDAY. FIVE SHARP!" they chorused.

Stacy, Joey, and Mick followed Joyce to her car. "Joey, how'd you do?"

"Great! I smacked the ball the tenth time it was pitched on my first turn at bat."

"He's getting better," Stacy said, thumping her teammate on the back.

"How'd you do, Stacy?"

Stacy shrugged. "So-so. I'd've done better if Uncle Ben had been here to watch. He better be here Saturday or I'm going to *un*adopt him."

"Is that like getting a divorce?" Mick asked, obviously intrigued.

Laughing, Stacy shook her head. "No."

"Joyce, how come mothers and fathers can get a divorce, but kids can't get divorced from their parents?"

"Laws are funny, I guess," Joyce answered, unwilling to get into a legal explanation. "You having problems at home?"

"Heck, no. My parents are always kissin' and huggin' on each other. How come Stacy can unadopt her uncle?"

"I can't," Stacy answered. "I just say that to get his goat. Makes him appreciate me. Maybe you should tell him that you're going to unadopt him. It works." She lowered her voice to a pitch only Joyce could hear. "When I say that, he hugs me until I tell him I'll never let him go."

"I don't think Ben cares if I unadopt him." Joyce squeezed Stacy's shoulders. "If you unadopt him, come to my house."

"Can't. I'd die and blow away if I didn't have

Uncle Ben to love." Stacy grinned. "Don't you feel that way, too?"

Mick tugged Stacy's ponytail. "Beat you to the car, slowpoke."

"I can beat you running backwards," Stacy taunted.

Both kids galloped off with Joey trailing behind them.

Joyce exhaled loudly. Stacy's question had taken her breath away. How could she tell Ben's niece that she'd cried herself dry since Sunday? It wouldn't take much of a wind to blow her away.

Between bouts of crying, she'd considered calling Mrs. Shane and leaving a message for Ben. Actually, several messages crossed her mind. Tell him I don't want him to coach; I never want to see him again. Tell him I'm a stubborn fool; we'll have everything his way. Tell him I love him.

What bothered her the most was that she knew Ben hated leaving her as much as she hated watching him drive down the street.

For a man who thrived on logic, that had to be the ultimate example of illogical behavior.

"As illogical as comparing me to Stacy's mother," Joyce muttered.

Did he consider any woman with gumption as a threat to his independence? What did he want? A doormat to wipe his feet on?

Joyce removed her car keys from the loop on her shorts. She'd cried and worried since Sunday

178

night, but tears couldn't dissolve their differences. She would adhere to her principles.

"I'll be damned if I'm going to a mindless idiot for the sake of love," she vowed.

Opening day for the baseball season Joyce hurried to the main field. She told herself she was nervous and excited about the first game, but her eyes kept searching the crowd for a glimpse of Ben.

"Excuse me, please," she said to the cluster of people standing at the gate that led into the field. Her heart lurched, then seemed to stop when she saw Ben and Bubba standing near first base. "Let me through. I'm the Astros' manager."

"Sorry, lady. No team mothers allowed on the field."

"I'm the Astros' manager," she repeated to the man standing guard.

"Yeah. Sure. Where's your team shirt? Nobody comes through here without wearing the right kinda shirt."

She waved her arms frantically toward her team. They were too excited over the trophies being put at home plate to notice her.

"You're not going to let me in?"

"Nope."

Joyce glanced at the fifteen-foot chain-link fence surrounding the ballfield. A mere fence wasn't going to keep her from where she be-

179

longed. She skirted through the crowd, heading toward the outfield.

Bubba saw her near-white hair and poked Ben in the ribs. "Where's Joyce going? You don't think she's going to chicken out at the last minute, do you?"

Following the direction of Bubba's eyes, he watched as Joyce shoved her clipboard under the fence. One glance had him sucking air into his chest. "Do you think she had trouble getting through the gate?"

"Yeah. That guard can be a ring-tailed polecat. He tried to stop me!"

Ben watched as Joyce began climbing the fence. Nobody and nothing could stop her once she made up her mind where she wanted to be. She'd go over, under, around or through solid granite to reach her goal. For some irrational reason, that thought comforted him. It should have confirmed his logical reasons for keeping his distance from her.

Slowly, he began walking toward her. He couldn't stop himself any more than a hurricane could keep from eventually hitting land with disastrous effects. His steps lengthened. He jogged, then ran.

"Joyce!"

"Ben!" She was halfway up the fence. "That stupid idiot at the gate wouldn't let me inside where I belong!"

"Come down. I'll talk to him."

Clinging to the fence near the top, Joyce looked down. Her head swam. A cold sweat broke out on her forehead. Her palms began to sweat.

"Can't."

Vertigo? Dammit, this isn't any higher than a high diving board. What's wrong with me?

"Joyce?"

"I'm going to fall," she muttered. "I'm going to be in the hospital while the Astros are playing their first game."

"Joyce. You aren't going to fall. Hang on tight. I'm coming over."

Squeezing her eyes shut, holding on with all her strength, she waited for Ben to rescue her. The wire bit into her fingers. She couldn't let go. She had to hold tight.

Ben shouted, "Hang in there, Joyce. The fence is going to sway with my weight. Hold on tight!"

Hand over hand, he crawled up the fence. His dark eyes flamed with fear, not for himself, but for Joyce. From the loudspeakers music began to play, but neither of them noticed.

Ben crossed over the top. "Sweetheart, you sure know how to get yourself into some outlandish situations."

Her grip slipped when she heard his endearment so close to her ear. Tongue tied in a knot of fear, she couldn't speak. She felt his hand cover hers. His fingers clamped around her wrist.

181

"We're going over the top, Joyce. I won't let you get hurt. Trust me."

"Can't move my hands. I'll fall if I do."

Ben moved closer. "Sweetheart . . ."

"Don't call me that. It turns my knees to Jell-O." She bit her lip to keep from blurting out her inner feelings. "Leave me here. I'll get over being scared in a minute or two. Go on back to the kids."

"I'm not leaving you hanging by your fingertips. Don't be obstinate."

"You're the one being stubborn. You know I can make it on my own if you'll leave me alone."

"Like hell. You need me, dammit." His voice lowered. "And I need you."

"You can make it by yourself."

"So can you . . . but every once in a while we both need a helping hand. During the week I've been gone I've felt as though an essential part of me was back in Texas."

Joyce squinted at him through golden-tipped lashes. She said, "You missed Stacy?"

"Yeah. But I missed a certain woman more. This is a helluva time to say it, but here goes. I love you, Joyce MacIntyre. When I get you over this fence I'm going to kiss you until both of us are senseless. I thought I was certifiably crazy when I left Texas. Nothing made sense. But I realized I'm just plain crazy about you." One arm circled her waist. His lips touched the crown of her head.

A hair kiss. Not a loud smacking kind that he gave Stacy, but one that was infinitely precious to her. Her heart slammed against her ribs. Her knees shook. "You wouldn't tell me that to get me over this fence, would you?"

Ben shook his head and promised. "We're going to win today. I don't care who plays what position. I don't care what the final score is . . . you and I are going to win."

"Ben, I love you, but I know I won't change."

She felt him pry her fingers from the fence and raise them higher.

"We'll fight like cats and dogs," she added, automatically raising her foot to a higher toehold.

"But think of the fun we'll have making up," Ben countered.

"I'll come up with silly ideas that you'll hate and expect you to back me."

"Unorthodox . . . never silly." He wrapped her fingers around the top bar. "Both of us are quick learners. We'll adjust."

"What if our team comes in last?"

"Sweetheart, it's just a game. Come on, get your other hand on the bar, then you'll be able to pull yourself up. We'll take a breather once you get your balance."

Joyce swung her leg over the top bar and straddled the fence, sitting on top. The music blared from the nearby speaker. "Are you going to marry me?" she shouted.

"Dammit, Joyce, I'm supposed to ask you," he

yelled. The music faded as he screamed, "Will you marry me?"

Perched on top of the fence, knees touching, Joyce answered equally loud, "Yes, I'll marry you!"

Thunderous applause accompanied with loud whistles and an uproar of laughter drew both their attention to the packed stands behind home plate. Ben and Joyce glanced from the grandstand to each other, then to the flagpole behind them. While they had been climbing, the national anthem had been playing.

"I think the eyes of Texas are upon us," Ben said, grinning sheepishly.

Feeling as though she were on top of the world, Joyce picked up his hand, kissed it, then raised it high and waved to the crowd. The Astros broke away from the other teams and headed lickety-split toward them with Stacy leading the pack.

"Witnesses. We're going to have to back down the fence, but you'll never be allowed to back out of your proposal," she teased.

Ben tossed his head back and joyously hooted with laughter. "Sweetheart, that's the first sensible thing you've said since I climbed up here after you."

"You aren't the only one around here that's crazy."

Stacy shook the fence with both hands. "Get down from there, both of you. What are you trying to do? Get hurt? I can't be the flower girl at your wedding if you're both busted up!"

"Can you make it to the ground by yourself?" Ben asked.

"Wanna race?"

Ben shook his head. He leaned close and whispered, "Later. I'll race you to the pool."

Bubba banged his spoon on his water glass and cleared his throat. "Attention, please."

Baseball season had come to a close. Parents and players had eaten pizza and rehashed the exciting games they'd most enjoyed. No one wanted the party to end.

"May I have your attention!" Bubba repeated.

Sonny stood up beside his dad. "Hey! Who wants to play first base at the next game?"

All eyes swung to Sonny. "See, Dad? It's what you say, not how loud you say it."

Bubba gave his son a manly hug. "I've got a speech here that I've prepared for today."

The kids groaned loudly. Bubba wadded the sheets of paper and started to toss them on the carpet. "Hey, Joyce. Do I have litter duty?"

Joyce grinned and nodded.

Bubba made a great show of stuffing the paper into his pocket, much to the delight of the kids. "There are a couple of awards I'm supposed to give to you kids. Joey, come up here."

Joey rushed to the front table.

"Our most improved player award. Ya'll remember how Joey got the hit in the last game that scored the winnin' run. Read what it says, would ya?"

The smallest child on the team raised the plaque high over his head, then brought it down and read: "I just live to feel those bases under my feet."

Everyone gave Joey a heartfelt round of applause.

"We have two Most Valuable Player awards. The kids voted three times, but it was always a tie. Stacy Williams. Son. Come on up here and read what yours has to say."

Stacy hugged Ben on one side of her, then Joyce, who was seated on the other side. She whispered, "I love you for making all my wishes come true." Head held high, she marched forward and took the plaque. "Mine says: 'To the girl who's a better player than most boys.' "

Sonny edged her aside. "And mine says: 'To the boy who's a better player than most girls.' "

Again the crowd applauded, but this time they laughed and nodded their heads.

"The coaches get awards, too. Mine says: 'Thanks for roaring like a lion and cleaning under the bleachers like a mouse.' " Bubba grinned at the team mother. "Ben . . . Joyce, come up here."

"Who was responsible for these awards?" Ben muttered to Joyce.

"The team mother. She seldom says much, but she has a wicked sense of humor."

Bubba handed each of them their awards. Joyce silently read hers and blushed from her toes to her hairline. Ben face turned bright red, also.

"C'mon Ben, read it out loud."

The room became quiet enough to hear a pin drop. Ben's melodious voice cracked as he read, " 'To the coach who starts the season straddling the fence and ends the season with a winner . . . the manager.' "

Joyce wiped at the tears of happiness caught in her lashes. She tried to speak, but couldn't. She handed Ben her award.

" 'To the manager who caught the coach, fielded the parents, and tossed the rules aside. Win or lose, we walk tall together.' "

Head bent, Joyce raised her eyes when she heard chairs being pushed back from the tables. Everyone was standing, watching her, waiting for her to say something, anything.

She glanced at Ben, knowing he couldn't say what was in her heart. Turning, she lifted the huge first-place trophy to the table as she tried to piece together enough words to say something other than pure gibberish.

She started with the first thing she'd heard at the beginning of the season. "We ain't gonna win no games?" Her hand slid down the trophy from the top of the golden bat to the spikes on the champion's shoe. "We gotta woman manager who's got crazy notions about lovin' baseball. She told us we're gonna win because we're the best." She paused, looking each player in the eyes. "We won the trophy, but I have one question to ask. If we'd lost . . . come in last . . . how many of you would play next season?"

Every player raised his or her hand.

Joyce raised a glass of soft drink in her hand for a toast. The parents followed her lead. "To the champions of the league, who never gave up . . . never said uncle unless they were calling Ben."

After they'd all taken a sip, the team mother stepped forward. "We just have one question for you, Joyce. Are you going to manage a team next year?"

Stacy piped up loud and clear, "She can't. Uncle Ben and Aunt Joyce have started a team of their own. She's gonna have a baby! Finally, *I'm* gonna have somebody to boss around for a change."

Bubba slapped Ben on the back as the parents loudly clapped their approval. "You ain't gonna let her manage a team?"

"Let? No one *lets* Joyce do anything. She decided she wanted to be a momma." Ben hugged both Joyce and Stacy. "I'm the mathematician, but she figured out how to make one and one equal four!"